The Ones

Who

Misbehave

By Hanna Lee

The Ones
Who
Misbehave
By Hanna Lee

ABOUT THE AUTHOR

Hanna Lee is a transracial adoptee raised and currently living in Kansas. She is a writer who speaks about racism and plans to continue to participate in anti-racism rallies. She continues to learn about adoption trauma and the policies in place that need to be dismantled. She also fights for and to bring awareness to the Adoptee Citizenship Act of 2021, to avoid anymore adoptees being deported. As well as furthering her education in Korean history and culture.

FOREWORD

Hanna Lee is a fellow Korean-born adoptee, and, like me, I could sense from the very beginning pages of her manuscript that she had something vital that needed to be said. Boy, am I glad I read on—that I followed my own curiosity—because after having just finished her book, I can tell you it's a worthy read. Take it from someone who rarely—if ever—reads fiction! As a reader and a writer myself since 1997, I've always been drawn to memoirs. You would rarely catch me with a fiction book in my hands. I felt I didn't have time for them; I would think, why read a made-up story when I already have a mind full of imaginings that I must contend with? Yet, Hanna's book is brimming with truth. And if you are adopted (and from Asia), you will recognize the inner turmoil and rage that comes with being lied to about who you truly are, thus not being seen for who you truly are; you'll connect with that deep emotion of injustice, and a part of you will be released from it as you connect with the protagonist's journey and her epiphanies.

The inner turmoil that one feels from not being seen and acknowledged for one's innate goodness is not just a minority issue; it's a human issue. Anyone and everyone will be able to relate to this story.

I'm honored that Hanna read the anthology my twin sister and I had curated and my memoir. As a researcher, you never know who the work will influence, if anyone. I'm so glad Hanna had the audacity to follow her curiosity and to reach out to my twin sister and that we get to be part of her journey.

I truly believe curiosity leads us to connections, and connections are the healing remedy for not only the adult-adoptee community but for so much more: humanity. May you find truth in this story. May you find epiphanies from your own.

Janine Vance
Of the Vance Twins
Americanized'72
Adoptionland: From Orphans to Activists

ACKNOWLEDGMENTS

First and foremost, I need to give a huge thank you to the Vance Twins and Adoption Truth and Transparency Worldwide Network. My journey began with buying a series of books to gain awareness and understanding of other adoptee stories. Luckily, I was able to find a plethora of amazing books because of Adoption Truth. During this time of connecting, I was met with nothing but open arms from them. They've given me encouragement and support that I can never repay. Janine and Jenette, you are absolute angels. Without you, I wouldn't be where I am today. Also, a huge thank you to Janine for editing, formatting, and all the work you did to help make my manuscript into a living book.

Secondly, I need to give a huge shout-out to the adoptee community I've found online. I've learned so much and grown into myself because of you. I never realized how much I wasn't alone until I took the first step to start looking. Shout out to The Janchi Show, Seoul Conversations, The

Universal Asian, and everyone else in the adoptee community making sure our voices are heard and our truth is told. Your support and presence are everything to me.

I want to take a moment to show some deep respect to the Stop Asian Hate movement for empowering Asian Americans. Allowing me to be part of something bigger and helping inspire me to speak up, stand up, and fight back! To the Asian community I found because of this movement, you are strong, you are fierce, and you inspire me with your passion! I will never forget the true connections I've made. The acceptance I've felt. And what it meant to stand side by side with my brothers and sisters, for the first time in my life. Shout out to They Can't Burn Us All, Asians With Attitudes, Real Asian Frontliners, Hate is a Virus, and all the other incredible organizations and individuals fighting to end hate and racism toward Asians.

A very special mention to my friend Moonie: Without you, I wouldn't have come out of the fog and began my journey. You started something all those years ago when you sat me down to interview me for your college paper. Thanks for allowing me to text you at any time and always being there to talk me through my anger and confusion. We had some really deep and meaningful discussions that helped form this story. You're an outstanding influence on me, and I am grateful for you, my friend.

I want to thank my devoted and amazing husband, Kasey, who has stood by me during my time of crazy writing this. I can't tell you how much strength I found just by the constant love and support you give to me every day of our lives together. I thought my life couldn't get any better than when I first started sharing my life with you, but you make me better every day. I couldn't be prouder to call you my husband, my partner in crime, and my best friend.

To my kiddo, Six, keep shining. Keep being absolutely,

uniquely, and stunningly you. I have no idea where this world is going to take you, but I hope it's to the very top of whatever dreams you hold for yourself. I will always do my best to give you everything in this world. To protect you from the hardships and hate out there. You're my whole heart.

To my friends and family. Those of you who have been here with me the whole time, where would I be without you? I'm fortunate to have so many people around me to stand beside me and encourage me. I couldn't imagine being able to have pulled this off without so much love and support from all of you. Brit, thank you for all the tips and advice you gave me when I began this process. I also want to acknowledge my cousins Erin, Christopher, and Marie, who I found through 23andme. You took a chance when I reached out to talk, and I'm grateful you did. My life is forever changed. And to everyone who has believed in me and told me to tell my truth, thank you.

Last, to my sister, Kristin, thank you for being so perfect, so I didn't have to be.

~Hanna

DEDICATION

To all the Asians victimized during the pandemic.
And to all those who didn't notice.

CONTENTS

Smoke

A fork plunges deep into the side of a full 32-ounce Styrofoam cup. As the prongs withdraw, they release four tiny streams. The fork stabs again with enough force to cause a fountaining explosion of caramel-colored soda.

A gentle voice says my name, and I return to the present. The memory dissolves like cotton candy in water. I'm sitting crisscross, my legs tucked under me, on an oversized white chair in the corner of my new therapist's minty-green office. The room is alive with a ribbon of thin fog. It visibly dances in the sunlight that's streaming in through the half-closed blinds. Left-over incense lingers from the last cleansing session. The room is cluttered shelves of insignificance. The dusty forgotten treasures probably once felt essential to buy in a fleeting moment. I resist trying to make sense of someone else's mess and allow my eyes to fall back to the person speaking my name. I feel my body vibrate, beginning from somewhere deep inside, and the feeling causes me to grip my hands until my knuckles turn white. I turn and lean forward slightly, indicating that I'm ready to begin. I know, to Dr. Cho, I appear to be sitting patiently with my hands folded in my lap. But inside – I'm seething.

She patiently repeats her question, "Can you tell me what brought you here today?" It's the standard first session question. I've had over a dozen first sessions; it's embarrassing to try counting them anymore. I take a deep breath and allow myself a moment to, 'Dr. Strange' the situation. In other words, I try to think of all the 14,000,605 ways this session could go and aim for one reality where everything works out. This conditioning method is how I enter therapy, a process that started over twenty years ago.

When I first ventured into therapy, others said I should think of therapists like magicians. These are the people I'm supposed to be able to tell anything to, and they help fix me. I quickly found out it's not that easy. Many of the therapists I saw over the years did not like what I had to say, and none of them could genuinely fix me. If anything, my bi-weekly visits only made me feel crazier.

"I'm here because I'm required to complete mental health treatment in order to keep my job," I reply robotically.

"Is that the only reason you're here?" she probes.

Dr. Cho's dark almond eyes hold a firm gaze on mine. I feel my hands trembling from trying to suppress my already rising tension. I shove them into my lap and curl into a corner of the chair, concealing them. Maybe it was the intense way her eyes refuse to break focus, or because they resemble mine so strongly, I don't know. But something inside me urges me to talk against my will.

"So...it was just a normal day at work. I don't even remember what day of the week it was, but I was going to lunch with five or six co-workers. I was super on-edge because I hadn't been sleeping, so I was living on Red Bull. We went through the cafeteria and got our food. I love Chinese buffet, so I got that for lunch. But so did everyone else!" I explain hastily. "And for some reason, the dining area was dead. Most of the tables were empty. There are like twenty-five big, round folding tables in the space. And it's always super loud from a million conversations going on, but today it was dead quiet. I got to the table and pulled out a chair to sit down. My co-worker was already there and he looks at my plate, smirks, and looks me dead in the eyes, and says, "Isn't all the food you eat considered Chinese food?"

I pause my story and steal a glance at Dr. Cho to gauge her reaction to this comment. But her expression remains unbroken by any indication of empathy, so I turn away, slight annoyance pricking in my guts.

"Then what happened?" she prods me to go on.

"I don't really know what happened. I just lost my shit, I guess. I must have dropped my food on the floor or something. I grabbed a fork, I don't even know if it was *my* fork, it was just *a* fork. I stabbed my co-worker's drink until the Styrofoam exploded. Then I just walked away, left the building, and went home. I didn't say anything to anyone. I didn't even think. I just had to get away."

"Can you identify why you were triggered so strongly?"

"I was just super tweaked out because of all the Red Bull, I think."

"I think the Red Bull possibly amplified the reaction, but it's not the reason you became upset. Why do you think this comment bothered you so much?" Dr. Cho challenges.

Imaginary quills bristle down my spine. I'm instantly in defensive mode. I've been anticipating this turn in direction. Therapists questions are so impersonal and generalized in a way that leaves me feeling an instant disconnection. As though a line is now drawn between us, showing me she's on their side, and I'm the only one on mine.

"So!" I snarl. "When someone embarrasses you in front of a bunch of people, are you supposed to just let that shit go? You know, no one is asking him what he did to cause this! It's all about what I did wrong, just like every other fucking time!"

I stand up and rush to the door, fuming.

"I want to talk about what he did, Van. Please come...Van..." her voice trails away.

I turn swiftly into the brilliantly white hallway leading to the main entrance of the Recovery and Wellness Center, my assigned residential therapy locale. Keep Hope, located in sunny California, that's what this place is called. With a name like that, anyone can become a believer. I make a sharp right, heading through the double doors and outside into the courtyard I'd passed through upon arrival.

My eyes dart around the concrete jungle, searching for my only refuge at this moment: a smoking sign. Several benches and picnic tables pepper the green park-like space, with towering gray buildings surrounding all four sides. Neat, slim lines of blossoming trees border the area. Each tree appeared younger than pre-school-aged children, waving their raised limbs like arms to the sky. Throwing tiny white petals to the wind.

A thin veil of vapor exudes from my lips, twirling above my head like smoke. I don't smoke traditional tobacco cigarettes anymore. I quit smoking for about two years (that was five years ago), but I started smoking again. My exclusive secret, I began to use a Juul. The little e-cigs that look like flash drives to me but became popular for smoking among the kids since the vapor produces no cigarette smoke scent. Therefore, I can get in my nicotine fix without ratting on myself for smoking again.

I take a long drag, inhaling deep. I take my time on the

exhale. As if all of the emotions I felt a moment before could eject from my body with a single breath. Out of the corner of my eye, I notice a bright orange figure coming closer. I pretend not to see, turning away slightly and focusing on the furthest thing in my view. A star, faded by a wisp of clouds in the sky but visible in the daylight, catches my attention. Footsteps approach behind me as I squint up. The next thing I know, orange is by my side. He's so close that his body pushes me over as his shoulder presses against mine. He mimics my body language, lifting his eyes to the clouds, searching.

"What are we looking at?" he asks, nonchalant.

"A star," I say.

I start to point where I'm looking but quickly drop my hand as he exclaims, "Who cares? That's boring!" and turns his back to shelter his lighter flame from the wind to spark up a joint.

'You're my new best friend,' I think.

I always feel more comfortable around people who move through life in a way that completely disregards the usual social standards of courtesy. Untethered to other opinions and free to exist unapologetically, these people embody a quality that I wish I could somehow take into myself. I've always been this way since childhood. Drawn to the outcasts in movies and books. The misfits. The rebels. The ones who misbehave.

Orange takes a wide, exaggerated step forward. He lifts his leg straight in front of him before planting his foot down, stepping forward, and spinning on his heel to face me full on.

"Why are you here?" he interrogates, nose wrinkled and eyes squinting in full inspection mode.

"Why are you here?" I retort, mirroring his intense questioning expression.

"I ran away from therapy," he says with his voice muffled from holding in a hit of weed.

"Me too," I say, "First sessions suck! But I thought you were referring to the bigger question like, why did the universe send you here?"

"Ah," he shrugs, "I'm taking a much-needed retreat from life." He points a finger gun at me and then jerks his hand back, indicating he's just shot me, and it's my turn to fess up.

"Well, mine's more of a forced break from life."

"Who forced you?"

"My work," I explain. "I lost my shit and caused a scene, so the hirer ups say it's either this or termination."

"And you came here?" he laughs while choking on smoke, holding the joint out to me.

I pluck it from between his fingers, "My only stipulation was to go to one of the most diverse treatment centers in the U.S," I pull the smoke deep into my lungs and hold the perfectly packed pre-rolled joint back out to him.

He waves it away and points at me to take another hit. "You're in the right-center then," he responds. "Out of the eighty clients here, they only allow like twelve of them to be white. Right now, there's only seven, I think."

"What about mixed-race people?" I ask, taking another draw and holding my breath.

"If you're mixed with white, you're considered the race that you look like to the world. You know that" he asserts, grimacing.

Caught off guard, I simply stare back at him as seconds tick away inside my head before I realize I'm still holding in my hit and explode with a smoke-fuming coughing fit. I was considering all the people I knew who were mixed-race and was aware they don't have a box on formal documents to mark multiple races. Those individuals would have to mark the box that represents the color the world sees them as without regard to how they personally identify. I was ashamed of this flawed system. And more ashamed, I had let the question slip out of my mouth.

Unable to think of anything sarcastically defensive to say, I dab at my watering eyes for a moment while taking him in. He's wearing a plain, bulky orange hoodie with black jeans and blue Chuck Taylor high tops. The sweatshirt is more of a burnt orange than a caution tape orange. His hair is raven black with wild tufts like feathers sticking out all around his head. Taller than me by a little over tip toe reach, his eyes resemble mine, but his lids seem less heavy and sleepy-looking. Sprinkles of stubble cover his narrow chin. And although he seems like nothing more than a stick figure in his oversized hoodie, I figure he can still take me in a fight.

"Can you get a weed prescription in here?" I ask, changing the subject.

"Dude, this place uses weed for everything. They hate big pharma and only keep a limited supply of actual pills here, for like sleep and migraines and stuff. You can even do Tripnotherapy, where you trip as a form of therapy. People say it works."

"I've heard of that. Psychotropic Therapy. Yeah, Gwyneth Paltrow had an episode on Netflix about it. Not super interested in that. So, this place is like hippie central? Love, acceptance, and drugs? I guess I don't know anything about it here, really. I just wanted to get away from home because nobody there gets me. And if they don't, 'get me,' how the hell can they be expected to be able to help me? So, I decided to try my luck someplace I've never been, someplace different and super diverse. But I didn't know that also meant weed for everybody! I like that better than being put on meds, though. None of the drugs they gave me ever worked anyway. They just made me crazier."

"This place is super cool," he says, "I've come here before

and always take a lot away, but this new therapist they gave me is just so intense."

He pauses, thinking. "Why did you leave your session?"

"I honestly don't believe in therapy," I explain. I've had so many therapists over the years. I have a complex about trusting them."

"Who'd they give you?"

"Dr. Cho," I answer.

"She's a miracle worker," he claims. "You don't know yet, but she's already fixed you. You must be a Korean adoptee then; she only works with other Korean adoptees since she is one. She was my therapist the first time I was here."

"You're an adoptee too?" I ask, my eyes widening with excitement.

"Yeah, I guess I should have started with that. It's kinda standard around here," he straightens his back and squares his shoulders.

His head lifts as he recites his memorized opener, "Hello, my name is Moon. I am a twenty-eight-year-old adoptee from South Korea. I am an only child, raised by a barren white family from a suburb of Missouri. Please allow me to tell you about my trauma," he smiles and trails off.

I smile back. I've never met another Korean adoptee who was raised by a white family from the Midwest and with trauma.

'We're the same!' I think. And I feel like I will never stop smiling.

Overload

I watch Moon's eyes focus on something happening over my shoulder. I turn toward the double doors, where several of the front desk staff hover. A sturdy guy with deep copper skin and a dreadlock man bun opens the door and steps outside. He's stopped by a hand from within the group, resting on his forearm. I strain my eyes to see who the hand belongs to when I realize it's Dr. Cho's slender fingers. Moon and I watch the people talk inside the doorway for a while before they disperse. Right before Dr. Cho turns to leave, she looks at me and nods, moving her gaze to Moon, smiling as she disappears.

"What was that? Why do you think she stopped them?" I ask.

"She's just really into space and time. Not as in like time travel, but space to breathe and time to figure shit out. She really did help me; you should at least give her a shot," Moon replies.

"Then why do you keep coming back?" I tease.

He backs up to the double doors, jerking his head in the direction of his movement to indicate that I follow.

"For the food," he says. "C'mon, it's almost chow time."

From my tour of the facility when I first arrived nearly two hours ago, I knew where to find the grub. I recall the follow-the-leader style guide escorting me around with short explanations as I tried to keep pace.

The ominous gray structure of the buildings did nothing to convey the warmth and wellness radiating from the welcome video. The cafeteria, which seems more like a "taste the world" themed buffet at Caesars Palace, was full of colorful stations indicative of the ethnicity of the food. Where the group therapy rooms convey whimsical "feeling" colors and abstract art, other rooms had chairs arranged in a large circle in the middle or pillows on the floor and overstuffed couches to lounge on. The exercise and meditation space are as basic as they come. Gym equipment lines the far wall in a room of mirrors, and next door, in a large, dimly lit room, mats and cushions cover the floor. Yoga mats are standing in a bundle, huddled against a corner. Inside, they diffuse essential oils into the air to inspire or calm, depending on how you are striving to feel.

Turning left and traveling further down the hall is the spa I would never use. I do *not* like people touching me. We decide not to waste time going inside and head toward the building that holds the client suites. This building is five stories tall and seems to tower over all the others. Each floor holds eight client suites and is a replica of the next. Upon entry, there is a large empty space that holds a desk occupied by two smiling guides. From there, you see three hallways branching off with rooms lining both sides. A bright sign protrudes from the white wall at the entrance to each corridor. The signs have words like – Aqua, Turquoise, and

Lemon to help identify them. Two hallways contain resident rooms, and the third holds therapists' offices.

Each oatmeal-colored residential suite contains two twin beds with nightstands, two small dressers, one closet, one full bathroom, and a new roommate – who the guide confidently claims I'd create an everlasting bond with to last our lifetimes. She informs me that my bags will be brought up shortly, and the tour ends in these rooms before she escorts me directly to my therapist's door.

As Moon and I step into the massive, echoing lobby, the environment feels completely transformed, going from absolute silence to organized chaos. A beautiful explosion of people fills the open space, filing past us to the cafeteria ahead. People of all different races, styles of clothes, languages, hairstyles, and perfumes that I had never come across overflow the space. They erupt with laughter and gleeful speed talking. The air sweeps across my body every time someone passes me, and I imagine this is how baptism must feel to a sinner in need of saving.

We slip into the moving crowd flow, taking baby steps with everyone toward the aroma of a meal. Many scents I recognize, but most I don't, and they flood my nose. Thick spices overpower my senses, but instead of allowing the experience to intoxicate me, panic awakens deep in my chest. I'm suddenly aware of the many different voices, languages, and accents that seem to swarm and surround me like angry bees. My mind races through the 14,000,605 ways I might not know what any of this food is. How would I know what to get? How do I know if I'll like it? What if it's my turn and I can't decide what to get, so I hold up the line? What if I don't like it, so someone thinks I'm being offensive and yells at me? If I try something new, what happens if I don't eat it properly? What if Moon leaves me to sit with his friends and I have to sit alone? What if I end up sitting by someone who doesn't speak English? Are there other Korean's here that will try to speak Korean to me, only to think I'm a complete fucking asshat for not knowing fucking Korean?

I wrap my arms protectively around my body. My head's down, and I'm deliberately hunched over to try to make myself smaller, invisible. I retreat inside myself. Without even willing myself to move, I step away from the line. I can feel bodies pushing in around me, and I take another step back. My eyes are still locked onto Moon's orange hoodie as I step back again and then again.

"Ow!"

"Oops, sorry! Sorry!"

I bump into a group of beautiful Indian women. They smile.

"You're fine, sis."

Moon turns slightly to say something to me, realizing I'm not following behind him anymore. My intuition says he's about to look for me. I briskly turn, weaving away through the crowd. I can't stand the thought of catching that questioning expression in his eyes that I don't know how to answer.

Once I was finally clear of the cafeteria, I had to focus to remember where my room had been. The Lavender Hallway? No, it must have been the Clover Hallway. It was eerily quiet in contrast to the cluster I had just escaped from, but the thrill of isolation brought me a sense of relief. My mind is running a slide show of the day's events.

I woke and packed. Standing at the window in my living room, a warm mug of coffee clutched against my chest, I tried to remind myself that time flies. I'll be back before I know it. What are thirty days in the span of a lifetime? My friend, Sam, from work, picked me up and drove me to the airport. I know they just wanted to give me moral support. Or needed an excuse to get away from their kids for a while. I waited over two hours to board because we got there so early. The trip felt long but wasn't more than four hours. I was on a non-stop flight, which I assume was to avoid allowing me to bail on a layover.

On the plane, I planned to play music that I thought would help pump me up and make me feel empowered. I created a playlist of upbeat songs, soothing rhythms, and motivational lyrics. Looking back, I should have listened to Kanye's remake of Daft Punk's song "Stronger" or Alicia Keys, so she could let me know how this girl is on fire. But instead, I felt Lizzo's vibes as she sang about taking a DNA test, and it turns out she's one hundred percent that bitch. I decided the more appropriate route was to embrace the emotions I was feeling rather than hide them, like concealer over the zit of false positivity. I wanted to marinate in my anger until the rage soaked into my skin and dripped off me like a repellant.

I scrolled through my Spotify until I found the best, most angry-sounding song for the job. When I saw it, I played Hed PE's song, "Waiting to Die," on repeat for the rest of the flight. It resonated with a message I wanted to invoke. That I don't give a fuck, you don't know me, and I'm not trying to hear the shit that you're saying because there's nothing wrong with me. I don't need to see things your way, so fuck you, fuck them, fuck everybody!

Silver Lining

I blow through the wide-open door to my suite like a breeze, throwing myself face-first onto the bed. My suitcase sits on the floor beside me. I want to bury myself under the covers, hoping no one will discover me for the next month. But as I hear the small squeaks from down the hallway heading right toward me, I know how unlikely this scenario would be. I lift my head enough to see gray and pink New Balances stop abruptly in front of me. The rubber soles of the sneakers did not get along with the overly waxed floors here. I lift myself off my stomach, turning to sit and look directly at the person in the shoes.

Her legs, the same size around as the largest part of my arm, are covered with leggings that I could only assume she bought from the Junior's department. Or possibly a larger size from the children's section. The black fabric holds a pattern of rain clouds and lightning bolts. Her t-shirt hangs at the top of her knee. The faded cobalt blue shirt displaying a giant Grumpy Bear print that gave the looker a hard stare with an expression of annoyance. A thick cardigan of gray and violet yarn covers her tee. The sweater's bulky nature mixed with the undershirt gave the illusion this person is shrinking before my eyes.

She carries a green lunchroom-style tray in her hands. The white plate holds a classic wheat bread turkey sandwich in cling wrap, a clear plastic cup of water, a bag of plain Lays potato chips, and a bowl of fresh fruit. The food rattles as her arms try to hold the tray out toward me. I spring up from the bed, grabbing the tray before it all clatters to the floor. With the weight no longer on her arms, she quickly folds her hands in front of her and steps away. I place the tray on my bed and slowly sit, trying not to jostle the array.

"Thank you," I say politely.

"You're welcome," she automatically replies, smiling.

Assuming her as an employee, I think she must have the job of bringing a tray to the new girl, not yet familiar with the cafeteria flow yet. But she isn't leaving.

"Do you work here?" I ask, unwrapping the cellophane and taking a bite of the sandwich.

"No," she giggles. "I'm Emma. This is my room too."

"Oh."

I quickly glance to her side of the room, but it looks empty. No pictures hang on the walls or stand at her bed. I see no sign of clothing lying on the floor or hanging from the half-opened dresser drawer. My new roommate doesn't have a sentimental stuffed animal happily perched against her pillow or a colorful throw blanket at the foot of her bed. The only indication someone lives in the space is an ornate silver clock on the nightstand, about the size of a baseball. I sneak a peek over my shoulder at my nightstand, where I don't see the same clock; I reason it has to be hers.

'What an insignificant, easily overlooked object,' I think.

At the same time, I notice a package sitting on my nightstand that wasn't there before. I put the thought aside to focus on Emma.

"I'm Van. Vanessa, but I go by Van. You didn't have to bring me food," I say innocently.

My stomach rings with guilt. Emma went out of her way to do this for someone she doesn't even know.

"It's fine," she says, "I remember my first day and how crazy it was at mealtimes. I didn't eat for nearly a week at first because being in that crowd terrified me. I would just grab a smoothie or a protein shake and then come back to my room. You're allowed to spend mealtimes and free time anyway that nurtures your mental health. It's better now because I know people from group. It just takes time," she smiles warmly, trying to convince me with her eyes.

Her hair brushes at the bear design on her shirt. The color of weak coffee, much lighter than mine, her warm brown strands end near the middle of her chest. Her eyes are deep honey orbs, wide and round. Emma's appearance matches the same ideal I had created in my mind for Asian women growing up. A petite, dainty flower, her skin warm but pale. The anime-style eyes amid hair so straight you never need to straighten it. By comparison, my hair was almost wavy – an embarrassment to the sleek black manes Asian women flaunt in the movies.

"How did you know I was your roommate? And that I didn't eat?" I wonder aloud.

"When a new person is arriving, they give the person who will share a suite with them a heads up. Show us your picture and stuff. Being suitemates doesn't just mean sharing a room here. It means we take responsibility for the other, making sure they're okay," she swallows. "So, when I saw you in the cafeteria, I knew I should go talk to you. But you left before I had the chance. I know how overwhelming everything is at first, so I decided to make you a tray and show you that there's regular food here too. Regular as in, classic American food", she giggles.

"Do you mostly eat American food, too?" I hesitate, unsure if my question is offensive.

"I've tried all the foods now! But when I first came here, that's all I knew. I'm a thirty-one-year-old Japanese adoptee from Nebraska," she says, eerily mimicking Moon's spiel only moments before.

"I guess I should have started that way, with the whole, 'the hello, my name is' thing. Anyway, I'm from Nebraska. My parents are white, and I had a sister who was also adopted, but she died when we were really little; she drowned, actually," her voice trails off a bit before she adds, "I'm here to work on gaining mental strength, but mostly, I'm just doing a lot of self-exploration about my culture and history," she smiles contently as she finishes.

I instantly connect to her, as though she knows me without even hearing my story. Our stories are the same. An adoptee from Nebraska! She was nearby the whole time, like Moon. They both speak perfect, unbroken English and started in the same place I did when arriving here the first time. I knew I wouldn't become uncomfortable around them because they were the same type of weirdos as me.

"That's awesome," I finally say, trying to act coolly instead of overwhelming her with the excitement of my epiphany. "I don't know any Japanese people. I don't know any people that are Asian, except my sister, but she's adopted too. So, not really Asian," I awkwardly joke, "That's why I came here, to immerse myself in diversity. I want to be someplace I would feel like I fit in or could be invisible. But being around all those people just made me feel like I don't fit here either. I don't know anything about being Korean. I just wake up looking like one every day."

Emma crosses the few steps between us. Closing the gap, she sits down on the foot of my bed. Her eyes filled with understanding.

"I feel that way too," her head bows with her confession. "I have made friends, but I know they won't talk to me after we leave here. I try my best to be successful in my treatment. I'm a good listener and work hard to be supportive of everyone; I volunteer to share in group and always write in my daily journal. But, I feel like people are only pretending they understand. Sometimes it makes me feel more alone. Like, they would rather agree just so they can get away from me."

"Right, God forbid anyone who attempts to open a dialog really be understood," I chuckle, trying to lighten the tension. "Hey," I say tenderly. "I think the universe made us roomies for a reason. It seems like we could be the same person. We aren't alone anymore."

Emma looks at me through the strands of hair in her eyes, and she smiles. I'm immediately ashamed for being annoyed by the idea of sharing a room with someone. I thought I needed to be away from everyone else to heal, but this teeny person was sitting here, as though we had been friends since grade school, and I didn't feel annoyed. I felt understood.

I open the chips and pop one in my mouth. As I chew, Emma wipes her eyes and fixes her hair. Her thin fingers comb through her hair to smooth it down. Dainty hands with French manicured nails and a pink butterfly painted on her middle fingers catch my attention.

"Your hands look like an anime princess's," I tell her, mid-chew.

She stops combing her fingers through her hair and puts her hand, palm out, and an arms distance from her face.

She giggles, "I've never noticed, I kinda do!"

"Funny story," I begin, throwing a grape from the fruit salad in my mouth, "Do you remember that movie that came out when we were kids, and the bad person transforms themselves into that beautiful woman and calls herself Vanessa? My mom would always try to point that out to me. Like it was such a great thing being named after the villain just because she disguises herself as someone socially acceptable. Like, see, if you look like a pretty white girl, you'll do just fine in life, even if you are a monster."

"I know!" she chirps, "I watched so many movies as a kid. I loved their stories and their songs. How the main character goes on this epic journey full of trials and tribulations. Meeting friends along the way that fight with them to defeat the forces of evil. Everyone learns a valuable lesson. And they all live happily ever after. But when I watch them now, it's like, there's a lot wrong with some of the messages they put out."

I'm exhilarated that she's immediately on the same page. She's also noticed these flaws in our society. It was like we were connected, a puzzle piece that's finally found a piece it fits with.

"Exactly!," I chirp, "like no one wants to tell a story to a child that's realistic to compare yourself to." As I say this, I am panning through all the animated characters I watched growing up. And none of them looked like me unless they were a 'bad guy.' "Did you ever notice that all the bad guys were dark-skinned or wore black clothes and the good guys were like all white? And even in shows where they are all the same ethnicity, the good guys were always just a little lighter-skinned—shit's racist. So, I always preferred the ones with talking animals. At least then, you weren't supposed to see race. Plus, I'm more like an animal than the strawberry blonde princess tra-la-la-ing through the forest."

Emma's laugh reminds me of a young child. It starts like a

baby automatic rifle, he-he-he-he-he-he, with a slow drawn-in gasp at the end. Hhuuuuuuuh. The sound is contagious, and I find myself nearly choking as I try to swallow my food.

"Some of the songs in those kids' shows were pretty awful. Did you ever Google any of the lyrics?" I inquire while we are on the subject.

"Noooo, like what?" she asks, her eyes wide with curiosity.

I lean over and lug my suitcase closer to me. In the front zipper pocket, I retrieve a journal. Inside are all of the thoughts I couldn't talk about with other people. The corners of my lips curl into a sly smile as I realize this is the first time I had felt safe enough to share any of these secret thoughts with anyone. I thumb through the pages until I come to where I wrote the lyrics. I open the book wide, handing it to her. Though the lyrics only include pieces from the song, Emma's face shows how the message is loud and clear.

Some of the lyrics spoke of the type of woman a man would want, obedient, hardworking, thin, and frail; others simply implied that women were a purchasable item for sale.

I watch her eyes narrow with satisfaction, understanding that she also deems these lyrics as offensive. A deep crease burrows between her eyebrows. In anticipation of her reaction, a surge like lightning races through my veins. Seconds tick by before her eyes look up from the page and meet mine. They're bright, with a comforting sense of disgust hiding in the background, matching mine.

"That's awful. What are women to them? They put those lyrics in a children's show? That's how Americans interpret Asians. That's how American boys believe Asian girls should be," she spouts, handing my journal back.

"I know, right?" I affirm.

"So annoying," she huffs before glancing away as if

remembering something. She looks back at me as she says, "Not to change the subject, but did you open your gift from Dr. Cho yet?"

She nods in the direction of a Robbins-egg-blue bag sitting patiently on my nightstand.

I reach over and pluck the colorful gift by its white string handles. My fingers search to locate what's hiding inside. I can feel a narrow item covered in a smooth, silky fabric. I pull the item out to reveal a white cloth wrapped around what I can recognize as being a book. As I begin to lift folds of the fabric, unwrapping, I see a design being revealed with black, red, and blue ink. I pull the corner up and let the item wrapped inside fall to my lap. I hold the cloth up by the corners: a miniature Korean flag. There's a pang in my chest. The symbols seem to be reaching to me, but I can't understand. I recognize the familiar images, but what it represents feels meaningless to me, so I look down into my lap and clasp the book. The flimsy cover is matte black, and the recessed print reads 'Jayden".

"Jayden?" I question, scrunching my face up.

"Read the inside, silly," Emma responds.

I flip the cover open. On the inside reads:

I named your journal because I want you to write as though you're talking to another person. Journaling can help create a sense of accountability. Please write every day, about whatever you choose. Consider this a free and safe space. In time, I hope you will begin to bring your journal to our weekly sessions and share some of yourself with me.

Dr. Odessa Cho

***

When I look up from the page, Emma is beaming. Like an ad for Orbits gum, I wait for a sparkling star to ping forth from her teeth and immediately disappear. She explains, excitedly, how her journal has been her mode of survival and how her journal, *Tiffany*, had been her only real companion.

"At first," she says. "My journal was the only person I talked to here. Without it, I wouldn't have the confidence to speak and open up with people."

Emma stands, grabbing the tray from the bed.

She let me know that she was going to run it back to the cafeteria before it closed.

Her hair sweeps side to side as she strides into the hallway, an air of glee palpable in her steps. I hear her walk toward the cafeteria, saying hello and how are you to every person she passes. They respond with confused looks in response that tells me Emma is typically not as talkative.

I pick up the pen that had also fallen out of the gift bag. I click the end and open my journal to the blank first page. Thin horizontal blue lines beg me to fill them with words.

***

Dear Jayden
This is Day ONE. FUCK YOU!

***

Storms

Footsteps sound down the hall, entering the room.

"You know, I learned more about diversity from children's shows than I did from life experience," I said, continuing where we had left the conversation.

My face drops immediately when I see Emma's flushed tear-soaked cheeks. She rushes into the bathroom and shuts the door. I couldn't hear her touch the door, but my intuition tells me; by the trademark squeak of her soles against the wood, that she is stretching her legs to wedge her feet behind the door to stop anyone from opening it.

I kneel outside the door, unsure of what to do. I use the tip of my finger to tap a light knock. Emma doesn't respond after I say her name. Or after I try to say comforting words, grasping at general terms that would hopefully apply. I finally decide I need to get someone to help in case Emma tries to do something crazy, like kill herself, because then I'd have to sleep in a haunted room. So, I calmly say through the door that I am going to get her therapist.

I dash from door to door, looking for anybody nearby. I check for other people in their rooms after the lunch break, but even the hallways are empty. Panicking, I head to the check-in desk and speak to one of the guides. She points me in the direction of the Clementine Hallway to a Dr. Kim Daniels's office.

When I reach her office, the door is closed. I notice the whiteboard that reads – IN SESSION UNTIL 1:50 pm. I glance around for the time and see a silver protruding rectangle clock with large blue glowing numbers that read 1:14 pm. I hesitate, but the possibility of Emma hurting herself pushes me forward. I knock on the wood door hard, scraping the skin off my middle knuckle.

The door opens, and Dr. Daniels gawks at me. Annoyance and alarm spread across her face. She appears like she's in her late 40s, so I think she's most likely in her 50s. Her hair is in a tightly twisted bun, accentuating her long, slender neck. Because Emma is a Japanese adoptee, I assume Dr. Daniels is most likely a Japanese adoptee. Their features are shockingly similar, the resemblance so close they could be mother and daughter.

"I'm so sorry. I know you're in a session, but I don't know who else to ask. I just got here today, and I'm suitemates with Emma." I take a quick breath. "And I think something happened. She's upset and shut herself in the bathroom. I don't know her that well, so I don't know if she would ever hurt herself when she's upset or anything. Can you please help?"

Dr. Daniels nods silently. She turns to her client and apologizes, letting them know she will return shortly. We walk back to my room. I try not to continue to ramble in an anxious panic. But that's what I end up doing. As we reach the Clover Hallway, Dr. Daniels stops and lightly touches my arm, indicating I should pause too. I look at her, curious to know what could be more important than getting to our destination.

"I should tell you," she begins. "I am aware of a situation that happened at the end of the lunch hour today. Emma has had an issue with one of our male residents who has attempted to hit on her a couple times during her stay here. However, Emma's shy and has also...experienced trauma, so she isn't comfortable talking to many people. Especially men." Dr. Daniels seems to be searching my face for any indication that I may already have some knowledge of my roommate's history but continues since I'm simply staring like a deer in headlights. "Today, that resident attempted to speak to her again, but she told him to leave her alone. He became emotional at this rejection and began to verbally attack her. Several of his friends made comments too. The things they said were completely out of line, and they are being dealt with."

"What did they say to her?" I press, my neck and face warming with frustration.

"They said racially demeaning things as well as sexually demeaning things," she vaguely explains.

"And everyone who saw this just let it happen?" I ask. My voice reaches an octave louder than I intended, a sign that I was getting angry.

"It was stopped within seconds," she reassures me. "But a lot can happen in a matter of seconds, as I'm sure you're aware."

She gives me a knowing look, and I don't appreciate it. I walk away because, in my mind, we don't have time to talk. My long, fast strides allow me to arrive at the door in half the time as Dr. Daniels. She meets me at the bathroom door, placing her head near an opening at the floor. She calls Emma's name in a gentle sing-song way. A few moments pass with no answer. I hold my breath, the tension in my body refusing to release.

Then, the heavy door opens just enough to fit a single piece of paper. Dr. Daniels speaks into the crack, putting her face as close to the opening as possible. She sputters, too quiet for me to make out a single word. Behind the door, sobs, sniffs, and broken whimpers cut through the darkness. I remember her face as she had left the room only minutes earlier. The aftermath of this attack is on the level of Pearl Harbor or 9/11 for us. The damage extends far past the moment itself. The real devastation creeps in because you never saw it coming. Nothing compares to the pain of knowing that you can never get away from the hate. When preparing to survive an attack at any given moment, every day is exhausting. We're fighting to survive battles we did nothing to start.

A guide from the front desk arrives in the doorway, looking puzzled at the situation. I don't know how much time has gone by. He turns to me with an overly toothy smile.

"Would you like to join a group session today or sit this one out since it's your first day? It's completely up to you, whatever you feel comfortable with," he directs at me.

"I think I'm going to sit this one out," I say and give an overly wide sarcastic smile back.

After nearly forty minutes tick by, and it's past the end time of the session Dr. Daniels had abandoned, Emma finally opens the bathroom door. She walks out slowly. Dr. Daniels embraces her tightly. She holds her, then shuffles them both to the door. Dr. Daniels mouths to me, 'We'll be right back.'

I nod, mouthing back, 'Thank you.' Then sit in the now too-quiet room, feeling flustered and angry about everything that had happened to Emma. With my legs crisscrossed under me on the bed, I grab the journal, open to the next blank page, and click the pen.

***

Jayden
This is Bullshit! Fuck today!

***

I scribble over the entire page, carving furiously deep ruts in thin lines with the rolling ball of the pen. I keep going until my scribbles and swirls nearly cover the page, digging the pen in until it had worn the paper thin enough to puncture through.

A knock at the door and a cheerful voice let me know dinner is about to begin. I realize I had fallen asleep while everyone else was in their group sessions.

I lift my head, peering to see if Emma's in the room. 'Just me,' I think. 'Maybe I can find her in the cafeteria and check on her.'

I wrestle my body, trying to get out of bed and move. I need to comb my hair and make sure my appearance is respectable before heading down. I flip the light switch before closing the bathroom door behind me.

Florescent lights wash my face out to a lovely shade of jaundice as I check out my reflection in the mirror above the porcelain sink. Creases line my cheek from the pillow. I splash cold water on my face before pulling my tousled hair into a messy ponytail. I stare at my eyes in the mirror. And I can see the resemblance to Dr. Cho's and Moon's eyes. And I smile at myself before exiting to put my shoes on and going to look for Emma.

When I reach the cafeteria, most people are already sitting and eating. The room resonates with chattering and outbursts of laughter. I allow myself to scan the sea of faces,

28

over and across every table, searching for Emma's.

Suddenly, an orange sleeve reaches up, waving spastically. I watch as Moon's face pops up from the crowd, both arms waving now. I nod at him and take slow steps in his direction, looking everyone over as I go. No sign of Emma.

Three empty chairs sit at Moon's table meant to seat eight. As I plop down beside him, I immediately ask if he's seen Emma. I tell him she's a tiny Japanese adoptee. He laughs and points to tables of girls that match that description.

After a rushed introduction to the four other guys at the table, he asks if any of them knew this Emma I was looking for. Marco, a long-haired Hispanic man with beautifully sculpted eyebrows, asks if that was the girl who got attacked at lunch earlier that day. While Ajay, a young Indian man, claims he only knew she had been taken to the medical unit in the North wing. The other two men at the table (Daveed and Ashe), I'm informed, are both Israelite guys Moon had met during his last stay. They don't contribute any information to the conversation.

"Why was she taken to the medical unit? Did they hit her or grab her or what?" I question Ajay with nervous anticipation.

"From what I was told, she wasn't physically harmed. I think she was just shaken up really bad. She's had breakdowns before," he continues. "Charlotte, who has group with Emma, told me that she told everyone that her adoptive mother was abusive to her. She would make her do all the housework and would beat her and refuse to feed her if she didn't do a good job and crazy shit like that; that's why she's so small. She was starved during her childhood. And Sheila, another girl from the group, told me she had broken down while talking about her adoptive father sexually abusing her since she was, like, nine years old."

My chin drops, and my hand automatically moves to cover my gaping mouth. My brain sputters, trying to process everything Ajay said. But it moves more like a computer screen that's stuck, a spinning rainbow circle in the middle, buffering.

I look at Moon. He appears to take this news very personally. I listen to his angry words arguing the disgrace of international adoption and saying adoption is child trafficking before getting up and huffing toward the double doors to the courtyard. I mindlessly follow him, still not fully able to grasp everything I had just heard. Ajay jumps up to join us for a smoke outside.

A group of people stand near the doors outside, circling several guys freestyle rapping in the courtyard. Cheers erupt amidst beatboxing and flowing rhymes. As we pass, I notice an Asian guy is rapping. He's tall, with a massive build. His hat sits sideways on his head, and his face shows an expression of confidence as his words smoothly spout. In his rhymes, he criticizes everything from the people passing by to the "Insult to our government that is Fucking Donald Trump!" Wild howls rise from the crowd entirely made up of African Americans.

We approach, about to pass by the group, when Ajay points to a handful of men.

"Those are the guys that fucked with Emma today," he claims.

Suddenly, my vision tunnels, and there's nothing else around me except them. All the voices are muted, and the only sound is the pounding of my heartbeat in my ears. I feel my neck flush, the heat spreading as my feet take me in their direction. Although my eyes are focused on them, the closer I get, I only see red.

Shatter

I hate not being able to sleep. My mind roams into the dark alleyways of my life. Sometimes I sweep into the past, where I suddenly find myself standing alone in an endless hallway during my first year at middle school, surrounded by blue lockers. The hallway is always so long it seems to simply dissolve into the distance. A rumbling of voices begins to build—the familiar sound of dozens of teenage conversations happening at once. Then the picture slows down, passing like a slide show on the ceiling above me. The audio seems to come from hidden loudspeakers in my mind rather than the people who are mouthing the words.

"FUCKING CHINK!"
"Get out of my school JAP!"
"Chinese whore, you love me long time?"
"Gook bitch! Go back to where you came from!"
I feel the pressure of the shove on my chest that forces me back against the lockers. Angry white faces are inches from

mine. An open hand surges forward, landing hard on my nose, fingers gouging my eyes before the bang of my head bounces off the metal. The hallway goes silent. Every set of eyes watch, and no one says a fucking thing.

The scene rushes forward – into the future - slows, then stops. I'm in a parked truck behind a fraternity house. It's late at night, and we're sharing a joint. He approached me earlier at school as I sat on the floor in the hallway, waiting for my next class. I hadn't noticed him, but he noticed me. His smile was wide, and he had warm hazel eyes. After the class ended, he followed me close, asking me to hang out with him later. So, I said sure and held my smile until he was out of sight.

As I snub out the roach, he grabs me and starts pulling at my pants, tearing them down.

'Oh my God, he's going to rape me!' I thought. But all he did was force me to get undressed enough to probe and penetrate me with his fingers. His left arm pressed all his body weight onto me, overpowering me and pinning me back against the passenger door. His right hand violated me. I'll never forget the constant look of disgust on his face as he conducted this uninvited exploration of my foreigner's body.

He stopped abruptly, scoffing. "My brothers were wrong; you don't have a sideways vagina."

The driver's side door had creaked as he opened it. He had stepped out and slammed it shut before retreating inside the fraternity house without a word.

I sit up abruptly, burying my face in my hands. Bent arms resting against my knees, drawn tight against my torso under the covers. I wish these memories would stop haunting me. I want to be able to sleep. I want to know if Emma is okay and if she's in a bed somewhere, feeling like this.

I let my fingers slide down my cheeks and rise to turn the bathroom light on. I leave the door open so the warm beams can brighten the room just enough. Sitting back down on my bed, I reach for Jayden.

***

Jayden

I hate my mind. Why can't I have control over this one simple thing? I'm so tired. I am so tired. Every day of my life feels like a fight against an invisible enemy that lives inside of people. How dare you expect so much of me. I'm the fucked up one. Why do I have to fix myself when it was everyone else who fucked me up? Why am I here, and they're out there? Why do they get to live content in the world untortured by the things they did that DESTROYED MY LIFE! I'm expected to be happy. But how can a broken mirror that's been put back together after being shattered over and over, supposed to be whole? Show me how to be happy. Show me how to be normal. Make me stop being broken. PLEASE HELP ME. I CAN'T STOP FALLING APART!

***

The journal falls to the floor. I curl up in a ball and turn my face into the pillow. Grasping it hard, I shake from the force of my sobs.

Daybreak

Sitting in the white corner chair of Dr. Cho's office, I wait. She silently clicks through something on her computer, her nose only an inch from the screen. I received a knock at my door before 7:30 am. The quiet voice telling me I am expected in fifteen minutes.

Several women are walking outside the office window, enjoying the cool morning air. I watch them passing by with brightly colored dresses and scarves. Some have dangling gold jewelry in their ears and noses. They're all laughing and chattering in their foreign tongues, with perfect eye makeup accenting their glee.

I had just begun envisioning the first of the 14,000,605 realities when my attention is drawn away at the sound of Dr. Cho's exasperated sigh. I turn to face her as she is walking around her desk to sit in a chair closer to me.

"I've been made aware there was an incident yesterday."

"With Emma? I know, where is she? Is she okay? Is she

coming back?"

She takes a moment and gently removes her black thick-framed glasses before looking at me and saying,

"Emma is with her therapist now and will be returning to group today. You'll have some time to see her after this. But I was referring to the incident involving you."

"Me?" I was taken aback. Confused, I ask, "What happened to me yesterday?"

She sits back in her chair with a look I can't translate. I instantly start scanning through the filmstrip in my head of yesterday. Looking at it all now, what a cluster fuck! Then it hit me. The look on my face must have shown my epiphany as clear as a cartoon light-bulb appearing above my head.

"Do you want to tell me what you think happened yesterday after dinner?" Her voice wasn't tense; it wasn't patronizing or even disappointed. It felt more like she was extremely curious.

Okay, I'll bite, I think. "I tried to kick the shit out of three guys at once...I think," I say, watching Dr. Cho's face very closely.

"You tried, but don't feel like you were successful?"

I was thinking, 'What the hell is she getting at? Is she tricking me into confessing something so cops can bust in here and take me away for assault?'

"I don't really remember what happened. Ajay told me that those were the guys that messed with Emma earlier, so I did what anyone would do. I tried to fuck 'em up, I guess. Like I said, I really don't remember. I was just pissed," I explain matter-of-factly.

"And would you say that this is a normal reaction for you?"

"My reaction to most things is a strong reaction, usually, I would say."

"Even when it comes to standing up for people you don't

know well?"

I pause. I was struck. Did I not know Emma? Was she not the same as me? Were her experiences not experiences I've had before? Should I not care about this person just because I didn't know her well? Why should it matter how long I've known her? I know perfectly well what's right and what's wrong. And getting messed with because she's a woman who wasn't interested and happens to also be Asian, that's just some fucking bullshit.

I lean in deep and look Dr. Cho straight in the eyes when I say, "I would stand up for a stranger if what was happening to them was wrong. And the fact that other people don't, doesn't show there's anything wrong with me. It shows there's something wrong with all of them."

She blinks and looks at me with a pensive smile as her cheek rests against her closed knuckles. After a minute or so is spent simply observing me silently, she begins to sit forward in her chair. She scoots until she's at the edge of the seat cushion and reaches her hand out, gently resting it on my knee. My body becomes rigid at the feeling of physical contact, but my discomfort melts away when I hear her voice say, very gently, "You did do what no one else has ever done. You stood up for Emma. You acted against men who could have hurt you, and you didn't hesitate. You're a fighter, Van. And if you keep fighting for the right reasons, I hope someday, with the right guidance, you'll win." She sits back again without breaking her gaze.

What was this? My initial reaction was to get angry and demand to know what she was trying to pull on me. My actions should have warranted removal, but what I was being offered now felt like a foreign concept. I'd never experienced this reversal of my behavior before. Empathy and understanding toward what she could see was masked by my anger.

We sit in silence for several minutes as I try to put my thoughts in a straight line so they can come out of my mouth. But nothing ever comes.

Finally, she says, "Kicking you out for expressing your feelings isn't what we do here. However, physical attacks are frowned upon, so let's work on avoiding those until next time." She rises, and I mirror her. Then she turns her body slightly toward the door and raises her arm to show me I am free to go.

I walk past her and into the brightness of the hallway, feeling like this was somehow in slow motion. But step after step, I could feel myself radiating in the profound realization that I had done something right. Maybe not the right thing, but for the right reasons. And for that to be acknowledged made me hate myself a little less.

Detonation Button

Emma jumps up from her bed as I enter the room. I rush over to her and ask if she's okay? Is she hurt? She promises she's fine now and laughs as she tells me what she'd heard I'd done to those guys that had messed with her. I tell her those assholes deserve what they got. I listen as she recounts the story, allowing interruptions of my angry outbursts, then I stop interrupting so she can finish. I tell her that we look out for each other now and she should forget about them because I won't let that happen to her again. Her brave smile shows me she believes me.

After breakfast, we walk into group together. The room is a gaudy yellow-orange with bright tapestries that hang in billows above our heads. Stretching from the corners of the room to the center, it was meant to give a sense of coming together in unity. Cheap metal chairs with nylon padding are arranged in a circle. Each chair is a different color of the rainbow and has been set up in rainbow color order around the circle. There's a total of twenty-four chairs, which equal four rainbows. I sit down in a blue chair, and Emma takes a seat beside me in a purple. Moon comes bounding in and sits down with enough force to scoot his green chair several inches. As he's re-aligning his chair with the circle, he looks at me, grinning from ear to ear, and teasingly says, "What's up Million Dollar Baby?" I give him a light nudge and tell him he's the baby; he's supposed to be my backup. He tells me he would have if he'd known I was going to go all Street Fighter on their asses.

My smirk quickly disappears as the rapping Asian strides in and takes a seat directly opposite me. I feel a flush in my neck that's quickly rising to my face, so I turn away, leaning into Moon.

"What is this group again?" I ask as I dart my eyes in the guy's direction.

"It's an Asian American support group. There's a group just for adoptees that we'll be in together too. But this group is for all the Asians' to be able to talk about their life experiences with racism or whatever. But it's supposed to help us all connect in our Asian-ness, or you'll find out." He cut off as the group leader's voice breaks in amongst the conversations. "Just don't punch anybody."

The leader is an older middle-aged Portuguese man, who welcomes the new faces into the group. He starts by asking the new members to stand and introduce themselves. A slender boy, much younger than me, raises his hand no higher than lifting it from his lap. The leader hands the boy a card and asks him to stand. With a quavering voice, he reads, "Hello, my name is…Raafe." He stops and nervously looks up, then over to the leader who urges him to go on. "I'm a twenty-two-year-old college student. My parents immigrated here from Lebanon when I was eight. So, luckily, I was able to pick up English pretty easy. We live in a suburb of Boston, where I attend community college. I guess I'm here because, well, I'm here to get away from out there," his eyes pan across a vast space only he can see the limits of. "I'm treated like a terrorist. And I need to figure out how to deal with that. Okay, thanks," he said with a weird hand wave before sitting down.

"Thank you for your bravery today," the leader says cheerfully as he scans the circle for other new faces. His eyes rest on mine, and he gestures for me to stand up. I tell him I would feel more comfortable remaining seated. He allows this and walks toward me with a card in his outstretched hand. I take it from him and read the instructions – Hello, my name is (your name). I am (insert age/occupation/race and a little about your family and where you live/are from) if you feel comfortable (add what it is you wish to work on while you're here).

"I'm not doing this," I say, not even looking up from the card. "I'm not opposed to sharing or giving feedback, but I don't feel comfortable telling everyone this stuff about me. It's not a natural way for people to...."

"BOOOOOOOO," suddenly erupts from behind the leader. He turns in reaction, and I can see the rapper guy slumping low in his chair, glaring at me.

"Who do you think you are comin' in here bringing your bullshit wit' you. Get the fuck outta here." He waves his hand in a backhanded brushing motion imitating shooing me from the room.

"Dakk, please settle down now," the leader gently urges as a light sweat breaks on his brow.

Dakk rises now as he speaks, pointing at me, "You know dis bitch attacked my boys yesterday, in front of everyone, and no one did nothing to her. She still here. If it was me attacking three females, sumthin' woulda been done, that's for damn sure."

I sit patiently, waiting for him to finish with a smirk stretching across my face. 'My turn,' I think, as the group leader is urging Dakk to return to his seat.

"I'm just one female, and I'm right here," I challenge in a tone of overconfidence. "If you or anybody disrespects a woman because she isn't interested, that's tiny dick mentality right there. But when your boys try to overpower and attack somebody with insults to their race, that shit's called racism. And your boys should get their shit together, 'cause I know, they know what it's like."

"Oh, and you some expert on racism?" Dakk scoffs. "You know about what it's like to be on the streets as a kid, taken in by black and brown neighbors cause your dad's in prison for shit he didn't even do? You know all about what it's really like, huh? I never even knew another Asian growing up. I didn't have any opportunities, so don't pretend like you know shit about it!" He reaches into his back pocket and pulls out an iPhone, which causes the group leader to start sweating profusely as he attempts to take the device. Dakk quickly turns his phone showing a screen with a picture of my white parents with my adopted Korean sister and myself, smiling out at everyone from my sister's social media page. "I sure as hell never had the kinda life that woulda set me up as a fucking doctor, that's for sure."

I'm shaking my head slowly back and forth, implying he should stop. But I couldn't say anything. The words were catching and collecting in the back of my throat, making it hard to breathe.

He continues to talk about riding our white privilege all the way to the top and how my sister was worth every penny my parents spent on her. She must make them so proud.

That's when I lost my shit. I jump up and lunge at him, immediately being stopped by Moon. Emma's trying to calm me, but I couldn't register anything she was saying.

"How fucking dare you! You don't know me! You don't know shit! You have no idea how hard my sister had to work to get where she is. The system is created for people of color to fail! Do you understand that? She had to bust her fucking ass harder and blow past thousands of her own people, just to be good enough to be selected for med school!"

"Shut the fuck up!" he shouts as he advances to meet me.

"Fuck you! How many Asians got into med school last year? Less than forty-two hundred in the entire country and she fucking did that shit too, mother fucker! Out of thirty-three-hundred million people! Four-thousand-two hundred Asians! That includes Asian Indians! How much research did you do before you opened your dumb fucking mouth? The world is built to make sure people of color are controlled and confined."

"People of color! You and your white sister aren't people of color. You fucking twinkies!"

"Oh shit!" Moon says under his breath.

"FUCK YOU!" I explode at Dakk. "You think our lives were easy," I scream as I'm wrestled by Moon.

After a couple seconds, I raise my hands to let him know I was done, that I'd calm down, and he relaxes his hold on me.

"Fucking banana bitches!" Dakk chimes at me. He's backing up to his chair, still spouting, "Yellow on the outside, but inside, you white as fuck."

His body's lowering to sit, and I dodge Moon's hand on my arm and rush over, kicking the chair out from under him. All I hear as I turn out the door is the sound of the metal clattering across the tile floor.

I know I'll be forced to process the situation later, but for now, outside in the fresh air, I feel relief. I sit beneath the understanding gaze of the smoking sign. I've always avoided talking about my sister. I try to keep my life as separate from hers as possible to avoid my messy one contaminating it. But thinking of her now, I just feel grateful she's in it. I'm so proud of the person she became.

I breathe deeply to slow my racing heart. I had made a stop by the dispensary in the Medical wing and was able to get some meds, which I was smoking now. I was feeling calm, my mind slowing down to a manageable pace, muscles loosening from their tense state.

A memory floats into my mind of a summer day in the '90s. A time when my sister and I were in grade school, both under the age of twelve.

We were home alone on a day I could only remember as yellow. The sun was bright and bursting through the windows, flooding the house with radiant light. We had only done this a couple times before and were still cautious of the danger that could come from anywhere. We were in the kitchen, perched on top of stools as we ate snacks and watched tv. There was a new episode of The Adventures of Pete and Pete, and we were zoned in when we were startled by the alarming sound of the doorbell ringing. We both turned to each other at the same time, breath held, eyes wide. "Get on the floor," my sister whispered. And we both slowly got down on the floor. Crawling in a line, she took the lead, and we moved our way across the kitchen. When we got to the wall that divided the kitchen from the living room, my sister slowly looked around the wall and out the front window, where you could see anyone who was standing at the door. My heart was pounding so hard I could hear it in the silence. She turned, rushing back to me on all fours.

"There's a man there."

"Do we know him?" I ask in a whisper.

She furiously shakes her head no. We could hear the

person shuffling on the porch for what felt like hours. Why weren't they leaving? We huddled together on the floor of the kitchen. Breathing quietly, I remember the way she looked at me and told me, "It's going to be okay," before squeezing my tiny hand with hers.

I don't remember what happened after that. How long we were there until the man finally left. I just know that there on the floor, surrounded by warm yellow light, she was there with me. My continuous lighthouse still standing despite all the storms. Always, the only person I could trust to tell me I was going to be okay.

Pastels

Deep breath in...and hold...release. We repeat these simple steps over and over in a dim room scented like minty grapefruit. I barely open one eye and glance at Moon through the sliver of my eyelid. My giggling shakes the cushion, so he shushes me out of the corner of his mouth. I close my eye and relax my face. A unified intake of breaths can be heard, then rushes of deep exhales.

Meditation is something I find extremely difficult. The first time I had the class, I couldn't get my mind to shut the fuck up. It raced all over the place, refusing to obey. I could put an end to one thought, but another one would burst out and shoot away from me, so I spent the whole class trying to chase and trap them. Luckily, Moon let me know that getting super high beforehand was his only salvation. We decide to test-drive his theory out on me. And for the most part, it does the trick. I can at least focus on one thought instead of a million. But still, can't quite, "still," my mind. It takes some people decades of isolation and discipline, sitting in a cave in the mountains alone, to become a master of meditation. So, I'm doing okay for my second time.

After class, we head to the courtyard for some air-scented air. Marco's on the bench next to the smoking sign. He has earbuds in and is swaying his head and shoulders as a cloud of smoke plumes away from him. He picks up his phone and turns the music off before removing his earbuds.

"I didn't know you could have phones in here. Dakk had one the other day, too," I say to Moon as we approach.

"Yeah, you can get phone time depending on where you are in your program. Only for, like, thirty minutes or an hour, though. Dakk probably had a phone he turned in and one he held on to. But, who knows how he has a phone. I just know it wasn't because of his good behavior," he laughs.

Marco chimes in that he heard Dakk had to have his room searched, and the phone he had was taken away. But he added he wouldn't be surprised if he had another one stashed somewhere.

"What were you listening to?" I ask after a second or two goes by.

He blushes a little as he turns the phone around and shows me the familiar symbol of a black star over an aged gold background. The figure of a man replaces where the top point of the star would be; his legs stand apart as his hand is seen rising over his head, finger pointing to the sky. I'm beaming, and I look back up at Marco, who simply shrugs.

I become an avalanche of excited conversation about how much I love Hamilton. The intricacy of the lyrics, the background dancers' movements perfectly encompassing every song. The simplest set capable of amplifying the moment of a single character or portraying an entire hurricane. The costumes, the characters, the message.

"I fucking love Aaron Burr!" Marco exclaims.

"He's not my favorite character, but he sings my favorite songs," I say.

Moon adds, "Thomas Jefferson is where it's at. He's hands-down the best character."

"What? The musical's called Hamilton!" I say. "The best character is Alexander Hamilton!"

"That's debatable," Marco jokes.

"And you *know* that Angelica is nothing more than a dirty homewrecker," I add.

"So was Hamilton," Moon snorts.

"Touché," I submit.

"I have to add," Marco giggles. "The real-life Phillip Hamilton – total fox."

Moon and I are cracking up. And I can't disagree.

"I think what I love most," I say. "The way women play men which is iconic given theater's history of originally only allowing men to perform. Playing women's roles in tragedies by Marlowe or the latest comedy by Shakespeare."

"That's so Queen Elizabeth," Marco sneers before adding. What I love is their support of the LBGTQ community."

"So awesome," Moon nods.

"Oh my God, yes!" I squeak. "And what about how they cast mostly only people of color. I mean, how fucking amazing! And I absolutely worship Lin-Manuel Miranda. I love that he made his vision of a more inclusive Broadway happen by writing musicals. And writing fucking rap into musicals, I mean, c'mon. Genius!"

"But guys, we can't forget the most important thing about Hamilton," Marco insists. "That this a story about an orphan immigrant, who came here and made himself, despite everything against him. He left his fingerprint on this country, and so can we."

"Rise the fuck up!" Moon cheers.

That begins a tidal wave of songs. Each of us singing out

our favorites. I start with the chorus of "Wait for it," while Moon takes on some of the more complicated lines from "My Shot." Marco does a compilation of "Satisfied" and "Say No to This" because 'those queens can sing,' he snaps. We go through the "Ten Duel Commandments" before getting up to head inside for class.

We are still singing as we stroll into Art Therapy. Classes are an organic selection based on how you're feeling. Here we can paint, draw, craft. It's pretty self-explanatory. We all sit down and start painting with watercolors on preset easels.

I ask Marco if he was into Green Day and knew about their American Idiot musical on Broadway. He and Moon almost crack their skulls together as they both look around their easels at me simultaneously. We are all around the same age, so none of us had escaped the Grunge/Punk/Alternative/Emo eras. And having all grown up in suburbia USA we all knew Green Day.

We talk a little about what we know of the music from the album, all remorseful none of us had been able to see it but definitely knew of it. How could it not have been epic with that rebellious punk music screaming emotions at you through performing artists? Songs that spoke about a nation controlled by the media and by hysteria. Songs about covered monuments and the broken American dream. The disease of society's willingness to overlook the downtrodden. What it's like living in a world that feels like it doesn't care about us and the heartbreak of feeling absolutely alone.

Moon says he's finished and brings his painting over to lay down and let dry. I'm painting abstract blobs and layering colors to make the lines darker. When I finish mine, I unclip it so I can lay it down to dry. As I place mine beside Moon's, he had painted a grenade almost transparently with lyrics in the foreground. They were lyrics from the song, "She's a Rebel." He tells me that it's for me.

I put it up on the wall next to my bed when I get back to my room. I smile at it for the longest time and try to think of how I could give him something back.

I snatch Jayden off my nightstand and start writing the lyrics. It took a while to fully remember them without the song playing. I hum the tune to myself while I find my colored pencils and begin outlining the letters. The designs and colors weave in and through the words until it wasn't just lyrics anymore, but art, like Moon had made for me. I tear the page out and read it over.

The words were from the song "Minority" and encompass Moon perfectly.

After I'm satisfied with my little gift, I fold it in half and put it in my back pocket. I open Jayden again to write a short apology for the violation.

***

Jayden

Sorry I tore a page out of you. That must have stung. Day 6 — need it for an art project. I had my second meditation class today and it was so much easier to concentrate when I was super stoned.

So, success!!! Did you see the picture Moon painted me in Art Therapy? Jealous? I sang Hamilton in the courtyard. Too bad you missed that because it was really close to Broadway caliber. Ok, I'm off to my next adventure. Ttyl

VAN

***

Flat Tire

Dr. Cho's watering her small plants that grow near the window. She welcomes me as I enter the room, and I instinctually walk over and plop down in the white chair that I've deemed as "my chair." She finishes with the plants and takes her normal seat across from me.

"Where should we start today?" Dr. Cho asks while her eyes are busy scanning my file for her notes on our last session.

"We had just started talking about if my adoption arrival was celebrated, and then we were starting into my childhood behavior as an infant and toddler," I recall.

"Oh yes, we discussed your adoptive parents telling you stories about how you cried inconsolably as a baby and how they didn't know how to comfort you because they felt rejected and frustrated by you. So, they isolated you in your room for this behavior." She looks up at me. "Which we see now was extremely harmful given the fact that you were an infant who had lost your mother, your life force, neglected in an orphanage, and then taken to a new world that was completely unfamiliar. Only to be abandoned there with strangers. All that to be misunderstood from the beginning and never given any nurturing by the people who had chosen to adopt you. The first two years are critical for bonds to be made between mother and child. How were you supposed to develop mentally healthy from an environment where your trauma was met with rejection?"

I'm not sure if she's actually expecting an answer to this question. I just knew that these realizations had sparked something new inside me. Not the normal anger that would manifest itself as explosions, but like a rain cloud that covered me and was washing some of the dust away and putting out fires.

My fingertips are tracing the edge of the seam on the chair arm. I'm inside my head, agreeing that what she's saying is the truth. Yet, I still can't see my parents as villains. A villain purposely causes destruction. My parents were just as much victims as I am. Aren't they? Who guided them through their experience after this child was handed over? This was all new to them, too, and there were no books talking about the trauma their child may have before they even joined their family back then.

"Van," Dr. Cho's quiet voice breaks into my internal seclusion. "Babies need touch. They need to feel connected to someone. Babies that come from orphanages are often left by themselves most of the day. So, when your adoptive parents found they couldn't comfort you, they also neglected you the essential touch necessary for that bond to be created." She stretches her hand out toward me, motioning as though she's going to rest her fingers on my knee. My body stiffens and slightly recoils in response. And she draws her hand away, saying, "I respect your boundaries, Van, but I need you to understand how this applies to your feelings of distance with your family? Of that invisible divide that separates you from them?" She pauses, and the silence makes me realize I'm holding my breath. "Alright, I'd like us to move into your grade school years now. Would you be okay with that? I think this will help you put your thoughts in order again."

I nod and begin to pan through the film strips in my mind from that time. I scan through birthday parties where I received gifts of fair-haired baby dolls and blonde Barbies.

In the class pictures where I'm the only dark person in a clump of children with hair the color of baby chick fluff, I can hear the photographer telling us to do a goofy pose. Several kids around me pull their eyes back tight, so they appear as thin slits. Their tiny cheerful voices spout, "Ching, chong, ling ling, ming, mong!" before an outbreak of giggles.

We're shining a flashlight against our turned bodies. We trace around each other's silhouettes on a large piece of paper hung on the wall. Mine is the only one that looks like an alien, eyes bulging at the front of my face instead of set back like theirs, and everyone laughs at me.

"Chinese, Japanese, dirty knees, look at these, Chinese, Japanese, dirty knees, look at these." The song resonates inside my ears.

"Van, let me in here. I can't help you if you don't tell me what you're thinking."

I bob my head and then close my eyes before letting my face collapse into my hands. "I don't know where to start," I say.

She smiles warmly, without a hint of condescension. "You

start wherever you want."

"Okay," I say and take a deep, cleansing breath in. As I let it out, I repeat, "Okay," and begin. "I grew up with white dolls and toys of white characters. When I was a kid, I didn't think about it much, but who are you supposed to pretend to be when you don't look like anybody on TV? Where are the role models and superheroes that look like me?"

"I had all the typical racist things happen, kids pulling their eyes back at me and saying dumb Asian-sounding shit. Asking me to speak Chinese for them. I remember one kid yelling at someone who asked me to do that, telling them, 'I wasn't Chinese, I was Korean!'" I smile a little at this memory. "I remember I was in Girl Scouts, and we had a sleepover at our troop leader's house. She had a make-up consultant come over to show all of us how to do our make-up since we were 6th graders and would need to look more attractive in middle school, I guess. She gave each girl a makeover, explaining what she was doing as she worked. Using colors that 'really brought out their pretty eyes.' When she got to me, I climbed onto the stool. Everyone looked so glamourous and grown-up. But she simply handed me a sample of black eyeliner pencil and said she wasn't sure how to do makeup on my eyes. And that was the end of it. The troop leader didn't complain. The other girls were busy looking at each other and themselves. I still don't know how to do my eye makeup," I admit. "I only know how to put on eyeliner." A single tear breaks free from the corner of my eye and falls. I look down and wipe it from my arm.

"Why do you think this makes you sad?"

"It just hurts to constantly feel too seen and invisible at the same time. My skin, my eyes, the flatness of my face are constant reminders of a world that wants to use it against me and as a reason to ignore me."

"And when these incidents happened, what did your

adoptive parents say about it when you told them?" She asks.

"I didn't even tell them about the makeover. Anytime I told them about things in the past, they made excuses for everyone else. They would say that the kids didn't know what they were saying when I was bullied. Or that I must have been exaggerating or misunderstood the situation. Always me, me, me, being wrong. So, I knew they would just blow it off. But I was a kid, and I was left to just deal with it. I just don't get why they never believed me. Why would I lie about that stuff?"

"So, you believe you didn't tell them about incidents that occurred later on in life after they had broken your trust in them? You couldn't trust that they would understand or protect you?"

"No, I knew that when it came to this, they just didn't get it. How could they? They've never had anyone treat them like shit because of the color of their skin or the shape of their eyes."

"Are you able to recognize the continuation of mistrust from your infancy? That there were repeated occurrences where they failed you? And therefore, you feel like there are these divides in your relationship now."

I sit for a moment processing everything. Then I slump back hard in the chair and claim, "I mean, I can now!"

"We're almost out of time, but I want to give you some books to read. Some are about the psychology behind the damage caused by removal from *our mothers*, as well as some other things you may be interested in. Other peoples' adoption stories. I think you'll see that you're not as alone as you think," she's moving along the bookshelves as she says all this. Grabbing a book and then piling them against her body.

Our mothers – that stuck out in my head for some reason

when she said it. Was she once in the same place as me? Had someone giving her these books to read as a first step? I had always known she was a Korean adoptee, but she never spoke about herself or if her experiences were anything like mine. I had so many things I wish I could know about her, but she always answered my questions with a question. I take the stack of books and thank her as I leave.

I unload them onto my bed when I reach my empty suite, looking each one over before placing them in a stack on my nightstand – *Adoptionland* – *Americanized '72* – *Master Adoption* – *Seeds from a Silent Tree* – *The Language of Blood* – *All You Can Ever Know* – *Inconvenient Daughter* – *Lucky Girl*.

Smiling at my personal library, I grab my journal and give Jayden some attention before I'm off to a class about Korean culture.

***

Jayden

I just had my mind blown off my head. I guess that's probably just what therapists would call a breakthrough. How did I live my whole life never thinking of any of this before? AND more than that, why is Dr. Cho the first therapist to talk to me about it? How could I let myself feel alone for so long when there were people trying to talk to me the whole time from the pages of these books? Probably even online, and I just didn't know to look! I don't know how I'll read all these books, but I need to get started! Anyway, I'm sure you'll be the first to see my notes. I'm nervous to start, but I think. I'm ready. Are you ready? Also, I don't hate my parents. We keep talking about my parents in therapy, but I don't hate them. I just feel sorry for them. I still have some shit to work out, apparently.

P.S. this is day 11/feels like I'm on Mark Watney time.

Van

***

Lamb

Our group leader is smiling way too big for this early in the morning when she exclaims, "Let's talk about relationships!"

A unanimous groan emerges from everyone except Emma, who is overly excited for most all groups. She can get me to crack a smile just by watching her eager face.

Today, we're in a room with painted Japanese Cherry Blossom trees bursting all around us. Their flower-filled branches are plumes of orange, light pink, dark pink, fuchsia, and lavender. The ceiling is painted like a daytime sky with puffy white clouds spotted sporadically.

This is the Asian Women's group. In a previous class, we discussed how women need to stop being so mean and judgmental of each other. The last one was about body image and social standards. I'm slowly learning the terms and phrases used in other cultures and finally feel familiar with all the different Asian ethnicities. Most of which I wasn't aware existed before now. As shameful as this seems, you have to realize, knowing this had never mattered before.

Just as the leader begins to speak, she is interrupted by the sudden entrance of a crazy-looking Asian girl. Now, it could be argued that we're all a little crazy here. So, let me clarify, I said *crazy looking*. Her hair hung in short chunks among long dangling strands. It was so purposely extreme you could have sworn she went to the Salon de Edward Scissorhands. Her t-shirt was nothing more than head and arm holes on a piece of pink swiss cheese. Even with the little bit of fabric there, you could see splatters of rust-brown blood. The black tank top underneath shouted – Slayer! And her jeans were torn in a way that made it obvious they weren't bought this way. The most shocking thing about her appearance was that half of her tiny face was covered in bruises that ranged from deep purple to yellowish-green. A sign that some of these were old and some were new. And, when she came in the room, she was laughing into the air.

We all look around at each other to see what everyone else's reaction is. Some have expressions of entertained delight, some have jaws hanging wide open, while others mouth, 'OMG,' with looks displaying how offended they are by the interruption. Emma's face is the only one that matches mine as we both begin to laugh with her.

The leader goes to the new girl and gently leads her by the shoulders out into the hallway, where we could hear whispers of a random word every now and then. No one moves from their seats despite the obvious curiosity. Instead, we all giggle and whisper to each other until the leader pops her head in and quickly informs us she will return in a moment.

As quickly as the leader retreats into the hall, Sunni bounds up to the middle of the room. She tends to dominate conversations in group with her cheerful comments and advice. So, it isn't a surprise she would use this opportunity to her advantage. She's a natural, never pushy or bossy, but encouraging. She's also in my Adoptee Support Group. She had been adopted from Bengaluru, India when she was four years old. Her adoptive mothers live here in California, where she was raised in a life full of acceptance and nurturing that stings my insides with jealousy. She's here to try to connect with other people from India, and she prefers spending time with them in person over reading or researching online. Sunni is someone I categorize as a *people person*.

"Ladies!" she clears her throat comically, and there isn't a straight face in the room. "Please, everyone, let's talk about relationships," she mimics the leader's shrill voice.

She leads us in several deep breathing techniques and asks us to clear our minds. Then we stand and swing the top half of our bodies down, our arms limply hanging as we hold the pose for four seconds before lifting ourselves up. Waving our arms in the air above our heads is supposed to symbolize the release of all the crap in our heads. We're being asked to close our eyes and think about something in our dating lives that affected us because it targeted our race. Choose one to focus on it to share.

Just one? – I look deep inside my mind and start scanning through film strips of my past relationships. How do you choose just one incident and know that it's the right one to talk about? Should it be the most extreme memory or one that's easy to digest? Scanning, scanning.

Kate volunteers to begin. Her story was sprinkled with tones of humor, teasing herself for always dating the white jocks. It was just what happens when you're a cheerleader, she explains. Kate is a Thai adoptee from a rural town outside of St. Paul, Minnesota. I had trouble relating to her because she said she had felt accepted and was involved in many activities during her school years. On the day she arrived to her new adoptive home, the entire town held a parade for her, and pictures were printed in the local paper. She always participated in social activities and fundraisers. In high school, she was voted most popular, most likely to become a celebrity, best hair, and most likely to be remembered. You get the picture.

After she had explained her dating past to us, she starts to focus on what happened after she graduated high school. During the summer before her first semester of college, she had arrived on campus early to start a student job at the university bookstore. The college had only been a forty-minute drive from the town she had grown up in. There was an older boy who worked at the coffee shop on campus, just outside the bookstore. They had talked casually on several occasions during her breaks but nothing more outside of that. He wasn't her type, she explained as her eyes became more and more focused on something distant, outside any of our views. Her story continues. Her fingers are picking at a loose piece of yarn, unraveling from the sleeve of her slim-fit burgundy cardigan. This boy followed her on her walk home after she got off work one evening. It was pouring rain, her place wasn't more than a four-minute walk, but she assumes this is the reason she didn't notice him. As she was entering her dorm, the boy must have caught the door behind her, she speculated. Her face was drawn now, hints of reliving the terror pulling her mouth back as she spoke. He had rushed up behind her as soon as she had unlocked her door. He had grabbed her from behind and forced her inside with his hand covering her mouth. He called her a Saigon whore and told her that he knew all about how she fucked his little cousin and all his friends. How they had made bets on who could fuck her next. Then he had licked her face and told her he didn't mind leftover Chinese before raping her on the floor of the dorm room. She said she didn't even remember it happening because she was so numb due to the betrayal she felt from her friends. All the guys she had been in relationships with had never cared for her at all. All the girls setting her up with someone new. Did they know? Were they in on it? She said she never told anyone about the incident. She just let it destroy her the whole year she continued to live in that room. She is crying now when she tries to explain that she felt like it was her way of punishing herself for being so stupid. She was humiliated and dehumanized. She believes it was her fault these things happened. How could it not be when she looks like a fucking Geisha? Then her words are replaced with heaving sobs.

Outpours of supportive words and hugs happen instantly. Kate wipes her tears as she lifts her head. Her words are strong as she explains that she had decided to come here a month after she left college. She was afraid of looking at herself in the mirror. But she smiles warmly at everyone now, grasping the hands of the women next to her as she explains that she knows that none of it was her fault. That she is a victim of racism and sexual abuse. And she deserves to move on with her life.

Soft claps fill the room. Some are brushing tears from their cheeks, and others say, *'Yas girl,'* but we all feel her story as our own.

Sunni was up and trying to urge everyone to quiet down and think about the impact of Kate's story as we share ours. Thanking her for her bravery, we press on.

"Who wants to go next?" she asks.

Emma shares a story disclosing that she wasn't able to have any physical relationships with men due to the sexual abuse she endured by her adoptive father. She focuses on her shoes as she speaks. Her attempts at relationships always failed because she wasn't comfortable in her body. She knew she would give away the terrible secret of her

61

abuse if she reacted a certain way to advances, so she simply avoided getting that far. Her voice is weak now when she hesitates before telling us that her dad was the only person who was nice to her growing up. He gave her little gifts and treats that they kept as secrets between them. As she got older, new secrets were kept between them. She worries about what her father would do if she wasn't his. She worries he would kill her before letting her belong to anyone else. Her only relationship experience had been the one she had with her dad, and quiet tears roll down her face.

I put my arm around her shoulder and pull her hard against my side. I whisper in her hair that she is my hero. The group rushes to envelop her with support. Surrounding and shielding her with their bodies against the invisible predator that holds her captive in her mind.

I hold my hand up without waiting for prompting. Sunni calls my name, and everyone's eyes turn to me as they move back to their seats. As they settle, I search for something to focus on while I speak. Today I choose a small green leaf that had somehow relocated here or magically fallen from one of the trees painted on the walls. I take a deep breath in and close my eyes. The only way to honor Emma's strength is to become equally as vulnerable as she is.

"I was with someone for almost three years," I begin. "He was the perfect partner. Funny, kind, smart, responsible, motivated. He was working and putting himself through college. He would bring me breakfast and coffee in the morning and was the only person my parents said: "made me better." But I always felt like I had to force him into things, and I used to hate him for this because I loved this person, I wanted to start our lives together. So, after two years, we finally moved into a little rental house together. I brought a computer and most of the furniture from my place. He brought a tv and a new set of pots, pans, and dishes. We lived together for about four months when I first noticed the file on my computer. He had gone to bed early one night, and I was looking for some pictures I'd saved. When I opened the file, there were three folders. Each one titled with bullshit numbers and letters that didn't make any sense to me," I take a deep breath in and close my eyes tight before going on. "When I opened the first folder, it was full of naked Asian women tied up on the floor or beaten and unconscious. Splayed out. I almost threw up when I saw it. The other folders only got worse," I continue. "The second one was hundreds of pictures of Asian girls being gang-raped. Half of them looked like they were fucking children. There was just picture after picture of different men fucking the same girl over and over. And then the third one was videos." My vision blurred from the tears collecting before spilling out, "All of them were Asian women. Some screaming or crying out. Others simply stared off, dead-eyed and disconnected from what was happening to them." My hands and body are shaking, but I'm determined to finish. I breathe slowly, trying to keep the heat in my cheeks from painting my skin. "I never confronted him about it. I was afraid of him—he was a stranger," I confess. "What's there to say when everything you need to know is saved on your shared computer? I mean, was this how he saw me? Was this what he wanted to do to me? To others? Did he see them as human? Did he see me as a human? I didn't know. So, in the end, I just packed his shit up when he was away to visit his sister out of state. I changed the locks and then left it all outside the door before I left to stay with a friend. I knew I couldn't handle being inside when he got there and found the bags outside, key not fitting in the lock, yelling at me through the door. When he asked for an explanation, I ignored him until he gave up trying to email or text me. I didn't feel like I owed him one. He's a predator. And I had been stupid enough to open my life up to him."

The room is quiet. I keep my eyes focused on the leaf. Finally, Emma's hand reaches out and rests warmly on my wrist. I look up and into her eyes that overflow with pain and anger for me. A strength growing inside me as I pan across the faces in the room. Each pair of crying eyes sharing with me that they felt my story as their own.

Cages

Sunlight is just peeking in from behind the closed blinds. Dark blue light is barely noticeable to anyone who hasn't watched this transition a thousand times before. I lay there syncing my breathing to Emma's deep intakes and exhales for a while before giving up on sleep.

I sit up and open the book that was left face down to mark my place. I read the first two books in four days. *Adoptionland* is a series of anthologies written by adoptees about their experiences. Their lives are summarized with a short story or poem. The second book, *Lucky Girl*, was about a Chinese adoptee's relationship to the biological family she was able to reunite with and how it made her life feel complete despite the struggle to fit into the cultures of her home country. My dive into them had become an addiction for knowledge—a look into a history I had neglected to acknowledge my whole life. I was reading a book written by another Korean adoptee now. Her search for her birth parents and the struggle with her adoptive parents to comprehend the hole she needed to fill. They had kept her from her biological mother, who had sent her a letter as a young child. They hid the truth about why she had been put up for adoption and the fact that her family had been searching for her.

Every page I read contains secret codes only I can understand. I feel plugged into a matrix that I used to be too ignorant to acknowledge but know has always existed. Now I can see that it makes up everything around me. Coding I see in one person that has sections matching mine. I absorb everything into my skin. Let it seep through and penetrate my golden flesh. I feel their blood in my blood. Their stories are mine to learn from now.

I get through six chapters before I can hear others stirring in the hallway outside our closed door. I dress quietly and go to breakfast, leaving Emma to sleep. There are days she stays in bed until the afternoon groups are finished, and I find her sullen in our room. Sometimes she'll open up to me, and other days she can't find words to describe the sadness that looms over her.

I step into the hall and pull the door closed behind me with a tiny click. Turning to head to the cafeteria, I nearly trip over the body sitting huddled against the wall. It's the girl. The wild one. I'd heard from Ajay and Marco during a smoke break that she'd been running amuck around this place since she arrived. I'd had my nose so buried in books I was missing everything. Looking at her now, she seems so small and helpless in her passed-out state.

Kneeling beside her, I give her a gentle pat on her shoulder. "Hey," I whisper. No response. I hold my breath, trying to listen for the sound of her breathing. It was shallow but audible. Good enough for me to abolish feeling guilty for leaving her there.

In the cafeteria, Moon cuts behind me in line. He already has a plate of pancakes and bacon but wants to see if I'll grab him a chia seed smoothie. The request starts with – "Your mission; should you choose to accept it" – how can I say no?

I join him, Marco, and two new girls at a table. Ajay was doing intermittent fasting and joined us for lunch but never breakfast anymore. I tear off a piece of bacon from Moon's plate before telling everyone about the crazy girl that had been sleeping outside my door.

"OMG, that girl is so extra," one of the new girls, Charli, was saying. "She tore the hijab right off this girl Dalia's head in International Women's Group. She pulled a bunch of her hair out. Everyone was just like, girl, you need to chill."

"What set her off?" I ask.

"Please, don't nothing need to happen to set her off. She just straight crazy."

Marco said she had all sorts of drugs in her system when she got here, but they put her in detox until she stabilized. He added that, from what he could tell, she may be more fucked-up off them.

"Maybe we should see if she wants to get high with us and hit up a Meditation Class," I suggest.

"No way!" Marco says, hands raised in a passive way. "I don't want to die today," and strides from the table.

The two new girls get up, laughing as they give another hard pass to the idea. I side-eye Moon and then raise and lower my eyebrows repeatedly before giving him a shove and saying, "C'mon, man."

We decide to take our morning smoke break before seeing if the crazy girl is still sleeping in the hallway. We sit on the bench under the smoking sign and light up pre-rolled joints. I tell Moon about the books I've been reading and this journey I'm finding myself on. He tells me he's read most of

67

those books, too, and it led him to start researching international adoption policies and starting support groups for adoptees. He's someone I'd consider an Anti-Adoption Activist, and I worship his passion. Before we head back inside, he warns me, once you learn all this, you can't unlearn it. Knowledge changes you.

The Clover hallway is vacant as we arrive. I feel a tiny wave of relief that the girl has moved along, but the feeling is immediately interrupted by the sound of something heavy hitting something heavier. Moon and I both stop dead in our tracks. Not breathing, not moving, just waiting. Another crash causes us to turn and look at each other before both following the same call to action. We surge down the hall looking inside open doors along the way. Nothing – there was no one there. Until I get to my closed door.

Moon's shoes squeal as he races over and abruptly stops by my side. I'm standing there just staring at the door, nervous to turn the handle. Voices inside. Moon flings the door wide open, rushing inside ahead of me.

I step inside and scan the scene. Emma is standing wild-eyed on her bed, hovering like an animal deciding if it should attack. The crazy girl is on the floor next to the bed and has stopped whatever was going on before we showed up.

I quickly rush over to Emma and pull her off the bed on the opposite side as the crazy girl. I glare at the girl and ask her why the fuck she's in our room. She starts yelling back at me so fast I can't make out what she's saying. Moon's standing in front of her, his hands up in a disarming way. While this is going on, I ask Emma if she's okay. She nods that she is, and I ask her to tell me what the hell is going on.

Emma starts rambling, "I was asleep but woke up when I heard the door open and shut. I thought it was you, Van, but then they got into my bed! And I got so scared when I turned and saw HER!" Emma was pointing at the girl as she

68

continued, "I jumped up and started kicking her until she fell on the floor. And she wouldn't leave, so I started throwing my shoes and anything I could find at her so she would go."

I knew this had been alarming for Emma after years of experience having a predator come into your bed, uninvited. I hug her and tell her that she's okay.

"This girl is coming off drugs and was passed out in the hallway earlier. She probably just wandered in and didn't know what she was doing," I say...

I can feel her body loosening up, so I release her from my hold.

I look over at Moon and the girl now, and they appear to be calming down too. I ask Emma if she'd be okay if we took the girl to her therapist, and she nods. I tell her to lay back down and try to rest. I'd be back soon.

Moon begins leading the girl toward the door. His fingertips are on her shoulders with his arms straight out in front of his body to make sure there was an appropriate distance between himself and this wild card. I follow them out into the hallway and give Emma a smile before shutting the door behind me.

Halfway down the hall, the girl is walking on her own now. Sullen and silent, she shuffles her feet like a geriatric in a nursing home, delaying my natural pace. I'm already in a heightened state of annoyance after seeing how upset Emma was and still hadn't been told why this girl was in our room in the first place. My frustration boils over, and I grab the girl by her elbow and start pulling her along faster. As quickly as my fingers make contact, she flies into a fit. Flinging her body around, breaking free of my hold before slamming herself against the wall and sliding to the floor. I stand there stunned, frozen with my mouth hanging open. I look at Moon whose expression matches mine. What had just happened was something I'd only witnessed in caged or trapped animals. Furious acts of lashing out and flailing in a desperate attempt for escape.

I knew this feeling and felt ashamed I had provoked her to this reaction. I slowly inch closer to her before sitting down on the floor beside her. I tell her softly that I'm sorry. I shouldn't have done that. I didn't have any right to put my hands on her. Her eyes flicker up to meet mine for a brief moment before looking away again.

"What's your name?" I ask her in a near whisper.

"Brella," she answers without looking at me.

"Brella, I love that. Like a shortened version of Barbarella, Queen of the Galaxies. Here from space to save us all." I say the last part in a voice that was trying to mimic an old fashion radio announcer and hold my hand out to her.

She puts her hand in mine, and I use the force of my body standing to pull her up with me. I ask if she wants to bail on groups today and hang out in the sunshine? Maybe let us get to know her a little better. This was the first smile she'd cracked since arriving here five days ago.

As we arrive within sight of the double doors, I begin to hum. Moon starts humming quietly with me, with smirks emerging at the corners of our mouths. We bust through the doors and step into the fresh warm air of the courtyard. White petals are swirling through the air in miniature tornadoes. Then we take off running and laughing like carefree idiots. Brella shoots off after us as we sing out the chorus to Scott Weiland's song, "Barbarella."

.

Glass

Brella follows us to our favorite place under the smoking sign. She's different now. Her face is slightly flushed from our run over here, and she seems more alive than I've ever seen her. She's smiling wide as she sits on the grass then falls backward, letting her arms and legs sprawl out. I light a joint and take a drag in before passing it to Moon. He takes a hit and passes it to Brella. This goes on for a couple rounds before I decide to break the silence that's growing more awkward in my mind.

"So, what's your story?"

She looks straight up into the sky as she speaks. "I'm a Chinese adoptee. I'm 29, my parents hate me and put me in here."

"Your adoptive parents made you come here?"

"They thought it would make me stop talking to my mother. They thought if they make me go to a place where I was around my own 'kind,' I wouldn't feel like I needed to continue to talk to her, I guess."

At this, I sit down on the grass beside her and can't help the questions that start pouring out of me. I have never met anyone who had actually been successful in this endeavor.

"You found your birth mother? How did you do that? How long ago? How do you talk to her? Letters? On the phone? Online? How did you find her?" My head is swimming. I want to know everything.

Brella takes a deep breath and tells us she hasn't told many people this stuff. But this is what she was here for, so she would tell us.

"My entire life, I felt like an outsider. I was treated like one! My parents had two kids of their own when they decided to adopt me. I don't know why they bothered, maybe to guarantee they would get a girl, who knows. Every time we went anywhere, people stared and asked my parents questions. And they would introduce us as 'their two children and their other child, who they adopted.' Never their child. So, when I was a teenager, I became more and more convinced that my mother was out there in the world. I could always feel this sort of pulling from deep inside me, and it was pulling me to someone or something. My adoptive family moved around all the time, which made it hard to make any friends. And every place we moved was just more of the same shit. White neighborhoods, white people, white ideas of who I am just because of how I look. I never fit in, never had friends, and just spent my time alone. So, I started searching online in my late teens, trying to crack the process of how to get my birth records from the adoption agency that brought me here. My whole life, I was told that my mother was a poor woman from terrible conditions and gave me up because she wanted me to have a better life than she could give me in China. My parents even told me they assumed she was dead just to try to discourage me from starting this search. But I could feel in my heart that someone was out there. I was somebody's child."

Moon pipes in, "Oh my god, the process of requesting your adoption file is so much bullshit! They charge you fees to give you information about your own life! We shouldn't have to fight to get our information. Why aren't we just given our papers when we turn eighteen in the first place? That should just be standard procedure for kids who are stolen from their birth parents and sold overseas, don't you think? I mean, if anything, so we can get access to our family's medical history, ya know?"

Brella says, "It took almost ten years to get anywhere. I reached out to people and would get a little help here and there but was mostly shut down by everyone I contacted. Finally, though, I was connected with an organization that helps reunite adoptees with their families. As soon as I met with them, I knew they would help me. Within two months, they had been able to get my file, reach the agency in China, and got my contact information for a handful of living relatives. And one of them was my mother." A tiny tear runs from the corner of her eye as she continues, "I reached out to her immediately, by email first, and then I sent letters. I heard from her about a week after I emailed. I knew there would be a language barrier when we spoke, but I didn't care. I just wanted to hear my mother's voice. I remember the first time we actually got to talk on the phone, all we did was cry. I want to go visit her so bad, but my adoptive parents are losing their shit over this! They just don't believe me when I tell them about what actually happened that forced me into being adopted."

Brella explains that her mother and father were engaged to be married and found out they were pregnant just two months before they graduated high school. Her mother was five months shy of turning legal age, which would have changed everything. She said they never had any intention of losing her. They wanted to get married and start their own family. That her mother and father had talked about getting work as soon as they graduated to make sure their child would be taken care of. When her mother's parents found out about the pregnancy, they took her out of school and put her in a monastery for "unfortunate women." Her mother's hair was shaved upon arrival, and she was beaten and forced to work day and night, scrubbing floors, cooking, laundry, sewing habits for the sisters. She worked despite being sick for most of her pregnancy. She suffered from debilitating heartburn due to constantly having an empty stomach, nausea, and vomiting. She was only given a bowl of watery porridge at 6:00am and two slices of plain white bread with margarine spread on them for supper at 4:00pm. On the occasion where the sisters would have a large donation, the girls would get a boiled egg. She said when her mother was too sick to work, she would get beaten as punishment for not being grateful to do the Lord's work. The girls were only allowed five hours to sleep a night, and they slept on thin mats lying side by side on the concrete floor. They were allowed to bathe once a week. She said when her mother went into labor, she was left alone on a metal bed. After four hours went by, her legs were tied into stirrups, and her water was broken with a metal hook. This made the contractions worsen, and she would cry out in pain. Every time she would be slapped by a sister who would come into the room and tell her to accept her punishment from God for being a whore. Twelve hours of this went on before Brella was born. At the time of her birth, she was named Dae – The great one. She said as soon as she was born, she was taken from her mother and only given back for feedings. Her mother was put back to work two days after giving birth. No medical attention was given to her torn labia. Nothing for her fever from an infection in her uterus. She wasn't able to produce milk because of this. She was told that she was an unfit mother and that her child would be given to better parents. She said she tried to fight them, but they stopped letting her see Brella. She could hear her baby crying in the room they left her in, day in and day out. After three months, her mother was told she had to leave, and she never received answers about her baby. She said her mother found out later that her husband's parents had signed the papers to allow the adoption to take place. She never even gave consent.

She said her father and mother reunited after her release and had two other children together. She had a brother and a sister. Tears pool inside her ears as she speaks. She says her parents had tried to go back to the monastery to get her, but they were refused to be allowed in. They tried to get a lawyer to have her released only to find out their child had been adopted and flown overseas to a white couple in America.

She sits up now, wiping her face with the ends of her sleeves. I want to hug her but don't feel like she would like that after her reaction to me touching her earlier. So, I just look at her and let my tears fall. I'm so angry for her. For her mother and her father and everything they all lost. So many people's lives fucked up when things could have been so different for everybody. She says she wanted to see her family, but her adoptive parents were furious with her and locked her in her room at their house. She said she tried to get out through her window on the second story and fell, cracking several ribs and bruising her face on a tree limb she missed jumping to. She then said after she left the hospital three days later, she had tried to steal her dad's car. She said they pulled in the driveway, and her dad got out, and she jumped over into the driver's seat and took off. She was able to start the car since it had a Push Start button and her dad was within range of the sensor. However, when she went to turn out of the drive into the street, she hit a pole because she was on tons of painkillers from the hospital. She hit her face but hadn't felt it. She said her parents got in their smashed car and drove her directly to this place and told her she was staying here until she "straightened up." She thought they probably assumed this was some sort of asylum or something.

She had used a folding swiss army pocketknife to try to cut her hair off on the car ride here. In her mind, she was standing in solidarity with her birth mother when she was taken to the monastery. But she was on so many painkillers she doesn't really remember doing it.

"Jesus, fuck," I finally say while putting pressure on the sides of my exploding head.

"Now, that's what I call a superhero's tragic backstory," Moon adds. "You've lost A LOT, but you've also gained the secret behind your powers. And now you know your back story. Which is more than most people get."

"For sure," I add, "you found your mother. How many people are out there searching their whole lives? Your mother and father loved you before you were born. They loved you, they wanted you. They fought for you."

She's looking at the grass as she picks at pieces with her fingers. "I found out my birth father died. Just a few months before I found them. He had colon cancer and tried to fight it for four years. It's just unfair that I won't ever get to know him. I'll never get to look into his face and see which parts of him are in me. I'll never know what it feels like to have him hold my hand. He spent his whole life searching for his stolen child, even when his body was failing. He's a superhero, not me."

This time, I didn't hesitate. I scoot close enough to Brella to put my arms around her shoulders and pull her into me. I hold her shaking shoulders as she cries and can feel her body melt into me as though she'd never been held like this before. And I rock her and softly sing the words to Barbarella into her hair because there aren't any words of my own forming in my head to say.

Time Bomb

I'm pacing back and forth in front of the window in Dr. Cho's office. Everything around me appears in a blur, as though I'm spinning in circles, only I'm not. I turn before I reach the wall and begin walking back toward the opposite side when I'm interrupted at the sound of my name. Had I not been talking out loud this whole time? She says I haven't said anything to her, only to myself. I refocus and walk to my chair, but I just stare at it and can't bring myself to sit down. I feel like I'm on the bus from the movie *Speed*. If I stop, if I slow down, I might detonate.

She asks me to tell her what I'm thinking. To help her understand what I'm going through. But I can't. I turn and start pacing, then I spin and sit down, stand again, then pace. And I can feel my entire body vibrating so hard my teeth are chattering. My hands are sweaty, and I wipe them hard against the sides of my jeans. My breaths become shorter and shorter, I'm heaving, I'm panicking, and I can't. I can't.

I'm suddenly being supported by Dr. Cho's arms around me. Her words are pouring out all over me. Her hands are brushing my hair and my face, and she's still holding me. She slowly lowers us to the floor as she feels my shaking legs begin to collapse. She's breathing in deep and then letting it out slowly, and I look into her face, and she nods, then takes an exaggerated breath in encouraging me to mimic her, and she lets it out. And I am looking in her eyes, and I begin to breathe.

After a couple minutes pass, we get ourselves up off the floor. She guides me to my chair, but I point to the couch before walking over and collapsing into the puffy cushions. I curl up on my side, facing the chair. Dr. Cho takes a seat across from me.

"Take your time. Whenever you're ready," her patient voice guides.

"I've been reading those books you gave me. And it's too much! Not just the books but like everything! Everything I'm learning from groups and hearing everyone's trauma. All these terrible stories," my voice was straining to get the words out. "I just can't believe all those things happened. I never would have known that there was so much suffering in so many different ways. And it's too fucking much!" I press my hand over my face before tears spill out in streams. "And I feel so guilty!" I bury my face in the throw pillow as sobs come bursting out of me. My whole body is heaving the more I try to get control over myself. Dr. Cho stands up from her chair and snatches several tissues from the box on the table before taking a seat on the opposite end of the couch near my feet. I sit up just enough to prop myself up on my elbow and blow my nose. Then I go on, "I just feel like I came here thinking I'm this beat-down shell of a person. Then I hear stories that are filled with so much pain. And I think, how dare I complain about my life. I didn't endure sexual or physical abuse by my parents. I was never hungry or denied anything. I was wanted, and I never questioned that. I've been given every opportunity in life. So, why? Why can't I be happy? Why am I just as lost as all of them? Why am I just as fucked-up when I didn't live with anything close to the fucked-up shit they've lived through?" I dab my eyes with the dry parts of the tissue in my hand. "And I read these books, and those stories are worse. When does it end?" I ask, looking directly into Dr. Cho's warm eyes. "It just hurts so much."

Then, Dr. Cho looks at me hard, and she says the most real thing I've ever heard come out of her mouth, "Your shit is your shit, and it isn't less just because someone else has more."

I gawk at her, shocked at the statement, before she just shrugs and says, "I heard it on My Favorite Murder podcast. It works."

I sit up fully now and face her end of the couch, "Do you think I belong here?" I ask, using both hands to rub the last remaining tear streaks from under my eyes.

"Yes, I think you were meant to be right where you are. Growing is hard; it is extremely painful. But you will come out stronger than before. You will take these stories and these experiences with you. And it's up to you to decide what you do with the knowledge you gain from them. I'm not encouraging you to keep going simply because it's part of the treatment process. It's vital for you to know that terrible things happen, but we can't change without stepping outside of what's comfortable. You have survived every trial life has thrown at you. Despite all the pain, you are still here, trying. So, what does that say about who you are?"

I wrap my arms around my bent legs and draw them in

tight before resting my chin on my knees. I still have this sinking feeling inside—a buildup of all the guilt I have allowed to consume me. I have a bad habit of making imaginary graphs in my mind ranking everyone's suffering. I feel like everyone else has a bar that reaches the highest line labeled, 'Super Mega Trauma,' and mine was just a stump. When I compare my life to theirs, it makes it difficult to believe I should be here with them.

All my life, I had been told what a lucky girl I was. Faces of white strangers looking at me after being told I was adopted. Suddenly all smiles as they would lean down to meet my child-sized height, "Well, aren't you so lucky to be here with your parents who must love you so much?" Their eyes would rise up to my parents' faces for a moment before continuing, "You should feel so grateful because your parents chose you to give you a better life." I would always be confused by this statement. What did they mean they chose me? And a better life from what?

I look into Dr. Cho's dark chocolate eyes and remind myself that she once started her journey in the same place as me. Not knowing where the path would lead but still moving forward, one step at a time.

"I'm very lucky," I state. "I know I'm fortunate to have been adopted by a loving family who has always been there for me. I know all of this, so why did I still end up here? No amount of love they gave me ever filled this hole inside of me. Am I ungrateful? Am I spoiled? Why can't I stop being angry?"

Dr. Cho repositions herself on the sofa. Turning to face me, she reclines back against the couch arm and sits very casually with one leg bent under her as the other dangles over the side. Her left arm rests on the back of the cushions. Her expression is pensive as she inquires, "What made you choose the word, 'lucky'?"

"I was always told I was lucky growing up."

"And why do you think people said that to you? What was it about you that makes you lucky?" she asks.

"Because I was told I came from a poor country, and my life there wouldn't have been easy. I would have struggled to survive, and…."

"And, yes, you would have experienced difficulties there, simply different ones. But you would have known where you belonged and who you belonged with. Do you think your life here is easy? Do you feel like you're struggling to survive? Those are the exact reasons you're here. Have you done any research on what South Korea is like current day? Or spoken to anyone who's visited?" she presses.

"No, I know that some of the stories I've read say that Korea is modern and prosperous. Wealthy. Not at all like those adoptees had imagined based on what they were told growing up in America," I say.

"And does that information make you feel like you were misled now that you've learned what the country is like currently?" she probes.

"I haven't thought about it, I guess."

She immediately rejects my ruse. "Just because we don't have something standing forefront in our minds doesn't mean it's not lingering inside of us. Causing us to have mixed emotions and the reason you feel conflicted inside. Your anger stems from years and years of repression. You never receive the answers you want, and the answers you got were vague and seemed made up. Am I right?" She's leaning in so far, I think she might fall forward.

I stretch back before leaning my shoulder deep into the worn fabric of the couch and rest my face against the back cushion. I wipe my sweating palms off against my jeans before saying, "I just don't understand why was I given up if the country is prosperous? Did the country change so much in the 33 years I've been away? I just don't get what was happening that my mother felt like I would be better off an ocean away from her?"

I felt deflated. As though it was taking every ounce of energy just to get the words out.

Dr. Cho sits back, patiently waiting to see if I'm going to continue. After several minutes pass, she says, "Van, there's no way to know what your mother's reason was. The only way you will ever know is if you ask her."

"Ask her?" I'm taken aback. "I don't think I'm ready to think about something like that. I mean, I know that some people have reached out and found their birth parents. Or even in some of those books, birth parents tried to reach their children. Like Brella," I explain, "she found her birth mother and family. She said it took her ten years. And I think it's great that she was finally able to find them. But she's also, you know, fucked up because of it. It would throw me off balance," I state.

"Elaborate on that a bit," Dr. Cho urges.

"Well, I think I'm overwhelmed enough, just with my life now. Trying to find a way to make everything balance between not upsetting my adoptive parents, keeping my job, and learning about my race. If I threw a whole other world on my plate, it wouldn't hold," I explain.

"It may if you got a bigger plate," she smiles at me warmly. "Our time is almost up for today, but I want to give you something to think about before you go. We are advanced beings Van, but deep at the root of us is a primal being with built-in instincts, just like all animals. When a baby animal is found separated from its mother in nature, it may be taken to a different place for a while to be taken care of by people. But once it's strong and healthy, it's released back to its own environment to be united with its own kind. Because even in nature, we recognize that a creature needs to be surrounded by its own kind to survive. It's natural; it's in our nature."

As I reach for the door, Dr. Cho adds, "Your world is as big or as small as you want it to be, Van. You get to decide. You never chose to be brought to this country. You never asked to be taken from your mother and given to new people. You have adapted to a life around you that you don't feel like you fit in to and therefore have no control in. But this journey is yours alone. And it's time for you to start being able to choose what you want. Take control over your life!"

Water

Jayden

We're on day 98162792308. Not really, it's day fourteen, but it feels like longer.

We were discussing the last book I read - Inconvenient Daughter. Man, that one really hit home. It follows a Korean adoptee through her teenage years into adulthood. Everything she tells us are mostly just moments and feelings occurring in her everyday life. But I recognize her anger and frustration. The way she lashes out and is repeatedly self-destructive are the results of trauma. That build-up over years and years of never feeling good enough, and no matter how much love there is, there's always a sense that you aren't the daughter your parents wanted. You're the daughter no one wanted. Why? Why do we feel this way? I've been feeling super down lately. Maybe I'm just overloading my brain too much. Or maybe it's exhausting to think of how many others are out there struggling right now, who's stories are still untold.

I feel like we should take a break from class today, Jayden. Let's go warm ourselves up in the sunshine! That'll make us feel better.

***

After a stop by the group room to let the leader know I'm needing an R&R day, I head outside. There's a sunny spot I like to go to near the South end of the courtyard. A worn wooden bench sits next to a large fountain that water rolls out from before collecting in a shallow pool on a tall tier. Once that tier is filled, the water cascades into the shallow pool on the tier below it. This goes on for two more tiers. All staggered so the water spills and flows as if going down steps. I've always found the sound of water soothing.

I take a seat and cross my legs, opening Jayden so I can doodle. I'm just finishing up with a rough Manga-style sketch of Emma's face peeking out from under a Hello Kitty hooded onesie when I hear footsteps trudging in my direction.

I look up in time to see Dakk appear near the fountain. My initial reaction is to panic, but I wasn't going to let it show. I close Jayden and straighten my back as he heavily plops himself down beside me, slouching low on the bench, his left arm resting limply in his lap as he places the other on the back of the bench. His fingers stretch out, and he uses the middle three to poke my shoulder and give me a little shove. I turn my head to look fully at him.

"Hey man," he says before reaching his left hand into his mesh basketball shorts pocket and fumbles around with something inside. He finally produces two pre-roll tubes and fans them out, showing one for me, one for you.

"Thanks," I say, a little hesitant as I take the tube on the right.

He pops his open and pulls out the joint to light it. Then

hands me his lighter, and I do the same.

After he takes a deep inhale and holds it, he side-eyes me before exhaling. Then he says, "I don't apologize, so this is as good as it's gonna get."

I snort and smile at this before replying, "I don't want an apology, man. I was kinda out of control for a while when I first got here. I have some issues."

We sit for a while just smoking in silence, and it didn't feel awkward or tense. I respect him for standing up for his friends. Whether they were right or wrong, he showed loyalty to them. I look back now and think of how many times I've flown off the handle in my life because someone messed with someone I care about. Even if they were in the wrong, it was about how many times they'd been there for me in the past, not about what they did to fuck up right then.

"I'm all for peace," he exhales loudly, "but some people don't respect shit but violence. You had me all fucked-up after that shit. I had to really re-evaluate myself, ya know? Cause like, at first, I was pissed, but then I had to have a sit down with my therapist, and we hashed it out. And, dude, look...I ain't never had an Asian community around me. I grew up rough, so like, I don't know shit about what it's been like for anybody else but me, ya know what I'm sayin'? And I came here fucking ignorant. But I get it now. I grew up in communities with black and brown brothers and sisters, and you grew up in a community with white brothers and sisters. So, we both the same, in a way. We both here to find who the Asian is inside us."

He pokes his chest several times as he says this. He's been looking out but not in my direction the whole time he's been talking. I've been staring at him as he speaks, watching his body language and hearing his verbiage. And slowly realizing that our environments had shaped us both to be who we are. We embody the people around us, the people who influence us, the people who raised us, the people who stood by us. And it doesn't make us any less Asian.

"I get it," I finally say. "And I learned something from you too. I'd never thought about all the Asians out there struggling. Not in a place to pay for their kid's college. I never thought about anybody out there who wasn't raised with the same things I had. All the Asian people out there didn't start out with the same opportunities. But I get it now," I explain. "It's tough to not belong anywhere, ya know? I mean, no matter what race the people are that you grow up with, it doesn't change the fact that we don't look like them. Sure, we can dress like them, talk like them, but we're embracing their culture and lifestyle. Where are we in that? How do you be Asian when you don't know what that means? Cause I can walk like them and talk like them and still get shit on because the reality is, we aren't them. We don't have people; we don't fit anywhere." My voice cracks as I say the last part, giving away my emotions despite trying to seem composed.

He reaches his fingers out again and uses them to sweep against my shoulder like a light smack before saying, "Why you acting defeated? How can you act like you giving up when I know you a fighter? You ain't afraid to come at someone for being wrong. You ain't afraid to stand up when no one else will. You here, working on your shit. And they out there without any thought about what life is like for us. Don't you fucking let them defeat you. You can always change your life. Look at us," his right-hand hits his chest, "we survive, we still here, so you better do something wit yo life. Be the change and all that shit."

"And all that shit," I repeat, nodding as a small smile stretches across my lips.

Lessons

Emma and I are lounging on the worn-out blue couch that sits in front of the TV in the rec room. The tired fabric reveals its age in the rich color that bulges out from its hidden creases when sat upon. The dark romantic navy that's been stripped of its vigor is now laid to rest here, with the rest of us. This room is shared by all residents in the Clover Hallway. Each hall has one room that's vacant of the standard suite set up and filled with several chairs, two couches, a flatscreen plastered on the wall, and a table with puzzle pieces sprinkled over the parts that have been completed. We're giggling as we sit close together and flip through a magazine. It's an issue of People's Best Dressed for the Met Gala. We turn the pages and poke fun at some of the crazy celebrity get-ups, joking that someone paid money to wear that, then immediately moving to, 'I would die to wear that.'

There's only one other person in the room with us, and she's busy watching an old rerun of Drunk History from a deflated-looking brown chair. Pretty soon Emma and I can't help but start watching along. How can you not when it's so hilariously entertaining?

The episode is all about Hawaii. The first story reveals the destruction that occurred during Captain Cook's discovery of the island of Hawaii. Since there were people living there, I wouldn't give him too much credit for his "discovery." The drunk historian's sarcasm, as he relays the events, makes it clear of his abhorrence behind the deaths caused by the invasion.

The second story is told by a balding man drinking gin. It starts with the bombing of Pearl Harbor and follows a young Japanese American man named Daniel Inouye. It explores the racism that began against him because of this attack. He was denied the right to fight because he was a 'Jap', the man reciting this tale stopped to insert that, "This was bullshit because not a one of these people have proven themselves to be anything other than loyal fucking Americans."

"Yeah, what the fuck?" I yell at the screen.

The story continues to show Daniel's chance came in 1943 to join and fight with the 442 Infantry Regiment. He fought with his platoon for two years, and during a brutal battle in 1945, he gets shot in the stomach but pushes on and ends up losing his right arm to a grenade blast. But then, this mother fucker, grabs the grenade that's gripped in the hand of his detached arm and chucks it into an enemy bunker. His regiment went on to become the most decorated unit in the history of the American army, yet the prejudice against him continued after the war. So, he went on to fight for change and became the first Asian American representative in the U.S. Congress. He saw that people like us needed representation in this country.

As I reach over to grab Jayden to tell him about this amazing story I had just finished learning about, Brella comes bounding into the room. This isn't her residential hallway, but she comes to find us here and hang out sometimes. Emma moves over for her to sit. They've made peace since the 'incident.' Her hair's been shaped into a cute pixie, getting rid of all the long hair that was still hanging all over her head. She'd refused a haircut until now. We 'ooooh' and 'aaahh' over the new look that she can somehow pull it off flawlessly, which I know I couldn't. The other girl in the room isn't looking at us but stares straight forward at the television, the expression on her face making it clear we're ruining her show.

We decide to clear out for her and start the stroll down the bright hallway to get to the courtyard. As we reach the main entrance, we come upon a new resident checking in. Normally there are always two guides sitting at the desk, but no one's in sight. Brella and Emma continue past her, but I turn to scan the halls for any sign someone would be returning to check her in. I approach her to let her know that someone would be here soon.

"Hey," I say. "I'm sure...."

"Uh, sorry, I don't speak Chinese!" the woman holds her hand up in front of my face, not looking up from her phone.

Her palm is lighter than her warm cocoa powder skin. She stands about three inches taller than me and has a thick high braided ponytail of the shiniest jet-black hair I've ever seen. Her lilac velour tracksuit matches her long acrylic nails that have to be at least two inches.

I'm stunned for a moment before I reply, "I'm not Chinese...I don't speak...I'm Korean," I finally get out.

She looks up now, well, her eyes look up, but her head is still pointed down.

"I – don't - care," she spouts. "Fuck you, Chinese bitches, always thinking you better than everyone else. Pretending you know the struggles, trying to put yo self with us. Bat eating bitches. Go back to your own fucking country."

Emma and Brella have stopped at the doors and are watching now. I'm sure they can hear all this, but I raise my hand just enough to show them to stay where they are.

"What fucking country am I supposed to go back to?" I retort, voice raised enough that she knows I'm on the verge of going off.

She looks up fully at me now and starts to say something, but I cut her off.

"No! Shut the fuck up! My fucking country – let me tell you about my fucking country. My fucking country shipped me here. They sold me like a god damned cabbage patch doll someone picked out of a catalog. And now, I have to fucking live here, with all of you dicks who don't want me here. So, do you think my white fucking parents taught me to speak Korean? Showed me where my fucking country is on a god damn map? Taught me how to cook Korean food and use chopsticks? Do you know what Korean money is even called? Cause I don't! I'd be totally fucked if I ever got ICE-ed back to my, 'country?'" I air quote. "Are you going to teach me all that shit? No? Then tell me, genius, where is MY fucking country? What the fuck do I have to do before you get it through your shit for brains that I don't have anywhere else to go. And no matter how much I, 'E-speeky-a-goo-engrish,' or no matter how much I dress like you, well not like *you*," I say, looking her up and down with an expression of judgment. "But I fucking live here. I work here. I fucking march in your protests. I donate to your causes. I fight for a race of people I don't even belong to and obviously am not wanted by. So please, I beg you, tell me where the fuck I'm supposed to go cause I'd love to get the fuck away from you!"

I spin on my heel and stride up to meet Brella and Emma, who are shaking from holding in their giggles. I give them a sideways smile as we step out onto the vibrant green of the courtyard, feeling like I'd gained some of my power back.

Hustle

Rumbling skies shake the tables as we're eating lunch. The sleepy fluorescent lights flicker and rattle high above us. This whole day has been miserable, starting with waking up to a pitch-black sky that's refusing to make room for the sun.

Brella had come bursting through our door sometime around four this morning. That first thunderclap sounded like the earth was smashing into another planet. It had to have awoken every person within a trillion-mile radius. I had sat straight up, gasping in panic. Emma had screamed and curled in a ball under her blankets. I called Emma to come over to me, but she was too afraid. I jumped mid-stride when the second one came, just as loud. Emma was shaking the whole bed when I sat down and tried to rub her back. Her quavering voice asked me to sit up closer to her, and I scooched the few inches and turned with my back against the headboard, stretching my legs out straight. She repositioned her pillow onto my lap before laying her head

95

down and wiping a tear rolling down her nose. I was brushing the hair from her face as the third crack came, and Brella had come rushing in.

She'd first ran and jumped in my bed. Then realizing it was empty, looked around comically, like one of those confused dogs you see on videos where a person holds up a sheet and then drops it, and they've seemed to have magically disappeared. She finally found us both in Emma's bed and doesn't ask before crawling in. Can you imagine the three of us?

Because everyone had been awake, the center decided to let us get up and start our day. Breakfast had been ready within thirty minutes, but we were all shambling along like zombies the rest of the day.

I was finishing my pho when Moon finally said something. We'd all been eating in silence, staring off in a daze of exhaustion and gloom. He and Ajay are at the table with Emma, Brella, and I. Marco had graduated a couple days ago, and that also added to the funk we were in. We'd all grown close during our days here, and his absence was a presence that felt like a shadow following us around.

"So, who's excited for therapy today?" Moon asks in a flat blasé tone.

All of us are slow to move our eyes from the spot they've been transfixed to. And we just stare at him for a brief moment before I pluck a fat steak fry from Ajay's plate and throw it at Moon's face. The smacking sound it makes causes Brella to spew water out of her mouth before sputtering coughs and laughing. Now we're all cracking up, and it's the first time I'd seen smiles all day.

Dr. Cho's at her computer desk when I walk in. She looks up as I'm shutting the door behind me.

"Hey Van," she smiles warmly. "What is up with this storm, huh?"

"I know, it's crazy. It woke me and Emma up, and Brella came busting in at the butt-crack of dawn, freaking out."

"Everyone's pretty much running on fumes today," she assures. "So, I want to get into current day stuff today. What's your life like right now? What's your environment like, your coworkers? We got into it a little bit last time when we spoke about your friends and relationships. But I want to build a picture of what a day is like for you."

"Well," I begin. "I'm a medical billing coder for a hospital. So, I have about forty co-workers with supervisors. It's a Monday through Friday job, and I'm off by 4:30 pm every day, so that's cool," I feel my hands starting to get clammy, and I'm annoyed at myself for feeling nervous. "Everyone I work with is really nice, and I get along with everybody, pretty much. Most of them I would consider friends," I say with a clumsy smile.

"Are you all about the same age?" Dr. Cho asks.

"Um, I would say there's a half/half ratio of people around my age and people older than me."

"Are there mostly males or females?"

"There's a good mix. I mean, it's mostly females, but there are enough guys that it's not weird for them or anything," I explain.

"And would you say there's diversity within the unit?" she asks.

I pause. I'm scrolling through the faces in my head in a sort of daze and focusing on the bookshelves behind the top of Dr. Cho's head.

"Van?" she calls me back.

"Uh, I'm the only person that's not white. But, okay, look, you have to understand that this company is very diverse. I see lots of people there that are Hispanic, black, Asian Indian, Middle Eastern. All the kinds of people. Gay people, trans people," I'm waving my hands in front of me, pointing out all the invisible people standing there. Couldn't she see the diversity?

"Why do you feel like you need to defend this fact so much?" Dr. Cho inquires.

"Because I don't want to give you the idea that I'm the only non-Caucasian person there. I mean, it's a hospital, it's big. And it doesn't matter that I'm the only person of color in my area. It doesn't bother me."

"But the incident that brought you here occurred at work, with your co-workers, right?"

"Yes, but I was just in a bad mood that day. It wasn't what he said; it was a joke," I say.

"And how many jokes have you heard like this one? Over the course of your life?" she questions. "From people you were forced to interact with and felt trapped in an environment with? Wouldn't that wear you down over time?"

"Regardless of how many jokes I've heard, that doesn't make what I did okay."

"You're right. It doesn't make it okay. But I want you to think about one thing – when people make jokes like this, who do you talk to about it?"

I'm thinking about this question and realize I'm glaring at Dr. Cho. My eyes are focused on her, narrowed and sharp on her face.

"That's not fair!" I spout. "You know the answer to that. Why would I try to talk about it?"

"Why not?" she urges.

"Because no one would understand, they would think I'm being crazy. And, honestly, it's embarrassing. It's embarrassing to have someone do that to me, and then worse when the person I tell says I just need to chill the fuck out, and half the time they think it's funny and laugh!" I exclaim.

I pull my arms tight around myself; I'd crossed them over my body as I was talking. I stare out the window as my top leg bounces up and down over the bent knee of the one propped under it. I'm visibly agitated, so Dr. Cho sits patiently, allowing me to cool down before pressing me any further.

'What a miserable fucking day this is,' I think to myself, exhaling in an audible huff.

"Van, let's move on from this. Let's talk about Emma. She's going to be leaving soon. We should do something special for her," she says gently.

I look back at her at this.

"Like, what kind of stuff can we do?" I take the bait.

"Anything you want. You want to order food in from outside or throw a party?" she asks.

"I want to have a movie night," I say.

"You got it," she says with a relieved smile. Clicking her pen before adding, "Give me all your ideas."

Warrior

"Shove that one over here!" I command, waving my arm to the center of the floor.

Moon stops pushing and gives me a hard look before huffing, then continuing to push the couch in the same direction he had been before I snapped my order. We've been given permission to move all the couches into the room with the cherry blossom trees painted on the walls. This will really set the mood. We're able to maneuver five couches into the room and have arranged them in two rows. Two couches in the front row and three behind fanned in a way everyone should be able to see the fifty-five-inch TV in the corner. A table is set up in the back for the food we're having brought in. McDonald's is Emma's all-time favorite! I ordered a spread of Big Macs, Quarter Pounders, double cheeseburgers, chicken McNuggets, and lots and lots of fries with sauce.

The movie is actually more like a watch party since we'll

be viewing the Kung Fu Panda trilogy. Emma and I had bonded over our love of cartoons and children's shows we love. So, what's more fitting than to end my time with her, watching movies that follow an adopted panda through his journey into self-discovery?

I'd been trying to cheer Emma up for a couple days. Marco's last day had been the start of her decline into uncertainty and anxiety. All I could do was assure her that she and I would be friends long after she left here. That I would bother her so much she'd get sick of me. And I promised her I would call her as soon as I leave here, and we'd meet up.

People are beginning to come in. The Asian groups that Emma had attended most are invited to share this experience with her before she leaves tomorrow.

"Hey, thanks so much for coming," I say to Dakk and Raafe as they stroll in.

"OMG, I'm so excited for Kung Fu Panda!" Sunni beams, clasping her hands together in excitement.

The room's getting pretty full, and I'm wondering where Emma's at. Brella comes prancing through the door and lets me know Emma's right behind her. Everyone in the room turns to face the entrance as we hear tiny squeaky soles coming closer.

Her face lights up at the sight of everyone. She slowly lets a smile spread across her face as her eyes well with tears. She'd grown so much during her forty-five days. I rush to her and pull her into the room by her frail fingertips. Everyone's around her now, clapping and cheering for her success.

"Congratulations, Emma!"

"You did it, girl!"

"Yay, Emma!"

"Woooooooo!"

"You're amazing!"

She's laughing and crying at the same time, and my only hope is that she can come back to this moment whenever she starts feeling alone out there.

Dr. Cho and Dr. Daniels stride in with large paper bags marked with the familiar golden 'M.' And everyone goes crazy in excitement over the surprise treat. Emma hugs me tight and starts bouncing up and down, still holding onto me. I'm being jostled so much my voice fluctuates as I tell everyone to dig in.

As we're all grabbing the food that's been dumped onto the table. Dr. Daniels fires up the first movie. Soon we all mosey over and find a good spot. Brella and I sit with Emma sandwiched between us. And the lights in the room flip off with a 'snap,' just as it begins. We 'shush' and giggle amidst the crumpling of hamburger wrappers.

As the picture spreads bright across the screen, you see Po, a panda, big and round and full of dreams. As I watch this all again, I'm seeing it so differently than when I'd watched it years before in theaters. But now, through different lenses, I notice the smallness of everyone around Po. How he's not only the only Panda, but he's also huge in comparison. A community of pigs and rabbits flows through the streets of his home city. And there are scenes where he bumps and bumbles through a world that he literally doesn't fit in.

Po's father is a goose who wants nothing more than to pass down the family tradition of noodle making. But Po's father's dream is not his dream. He fantasizes about being a great Kung Fu warrior but hides this from his father in order to not disappoint him. This is the equivalent of adoptive parents teaching you their family traditions, not regarding traditions that teach us about our own. Expectations of us following in their footsteps instead of choosing our own paths. Wanting us to learn from them instead of trying harder to learn from us.

The day arrives of great celebration as the entire city races to watch the ceremony selecting the Dragon Warrior, including the Furious Five. Po sneaks there, telling his father he's going to sell noodles. Long story short, Po's father finds him trying to sneak into the ceremony; Po ends up being shot into the sky by a bunch of fireworks and lands in front of Oogway's finger, selecting him as the Dragon Warrior.

Arriving at the Jade Palace, Po soon realizes, despite being in the place he's always felt he belongs, he isn't accepted here either. His new compatriots reject him, bullying him, and are quick to show their disapproval for his presence. Even his Master, Shifu, ridicules him endlessly. But Po doesn't give up. Even when he begins to feel doubts, he stays true to himself and pushes on. This made me think back to the times I had felt rejected by Asians. Even though I felt I should have belonged with them, I was something else to them. A faux Asian, given away by the way I spoke and the white parents that were at my side. I watch Po take beating after beating during his training. Each one he takes in stride, never letting it defeat him.

What really hit me, though, was when Shifu believes they've run Po off and, in searching for him, finds him eating peaches from the 'Sacred Peach Tree.'

Po explains, "I stayed because every time you threw a brick at my head or said I smelled, it hurt! But it could never hurt more than it did every day of my life just being me."

And that really hit me. That it hurts having to get out of my comfort zone, to grow and learn things I may not have been ready for. But none of the things I've put myself through here have hurt any more than living every day of my life just being me. Right on, Kung Fu Panda, right on!

Soon Po has completed his training and is ready to receive the dragon scroll. Upon opening it, one's said to be able to see light in the deepest cave and feel the universe in motion around them. When Po opens it, he just sees his own face, reflecting off a shiny golden page. After this, Shifu and the others don't know how they'll ever defeat the dangerous Tai Lung, a disgruntled former student to Shifu, who's approaching the city.

Po returns to his father on the streets of the city, as everyone tries to evacuate. His dad encourages Po to just be 'noodle folk.' When Po doesn't understand how their dreams can be so different, his father tries to cheer him up by telling him the secret ingredient in their family's 'secret ingredient soup.'

"There is no secret ingredient - to make something special, you just have to believe it's special."

I glance over at Emma for the first time since we started watching. She's smiling with a tear beginning to make its way down her cheek. I pat her knee softly. Po defeats Tai Lung with the new confidence he's found in himself. And the moral of the story is to be true to yourself, no matter how much it hurts. I don't know if that's really the moral, but that's what it said to me.

Everyone groans as the movie ends, and we stretch our legs. Some walk over to grab the cold but still good left-over food on the table. Some use the restroom or go to grab a soda from the cafeteria. Emma's gleefully chatting with a couple people standing around her. And I'm starting to struggle with the idea that by this time tomorrow, she'll be gone. The thought is broken at the sight of Brella's face, suddenly inches from mine. She lunges in and embraces me, forcing us both to stumble to regain balance.

"This is so much fun!" she squeals. And I giggle, glad everyone seems to be enjoying the movies I chose. People are all smiles as they return to the room. And I glance over at Emma, who's laughing her trademark laugh.

Winds

As we begin the second movie, the lights click off. Po's relationship with his father begins to feel strained after he has flashbacks that invade his dreams and his waking hours. When he tells his father about these visions, Po's father reluctantly tells him that he's adopted. And though Po had already known this fact, he wondered why he'd never been told before.

Oogway is trying to become a master of 'Inner Peace,' and in turn, Po also tries to teach himself. On a mission, he dreams of his mother abandoning him and feels discouraged, believing his parents didn't want him. These visions begin to grow and form more clearly. And the distraction causes the villainous Shen to escape. The Furious Five find it hard to trust Po without him being willing to talk about what's going on. And he is forced to admit that he needs to find answers to what these visions mean, and he needs to find out who he is. Which is pretty much what we're all trying to do here at this center. There is a notable moment when Shen tries to manipulate Po by asking him.

"You think knowing will heal you? Fill some crater in your soul?"

And that's the voice of self-doubt that I've heard in my mind a million times on this journey. The voice that tries to keep you safe in the bubble you've kept yourself in your whole life. So, fuck you, Shen. Po will help me defeat you! I glance around to take in everyone's faces. Softly glowing hues change colors on their skin as scenes move. Everyone's eyes are fixed on the images. I turn back around, smiling to myself.

Po is eventually able to recall his story of Shen attacking his village and his mother hiding him in a crate of radishes so that he could survive. As the village around them burns. Knowing his story, he can find 'Inner Peace.' In the end, Shen asks.

"How did you find peace? I took everything from you?"

To which Po simply replies, "You've gotta let go of that stuff from the past because it just doesn't matter! The only thing that matters is what you choose to be now."

And that's the moral of this story! He nails it!

Lights click on, and we groan and shield our eyes like vampires exposed to sunlight. Several people get up to use the bathroom or grab snacks. I stand up and stretch my arms up, fingertips pointed and reaching to the ceiling. Brella pokes my stomach, laughing, and I hunch over dramatically – pretending she'd just sucker-punched me. Emma rolls back on the couch, clutching her stomach in laugher.

'This is perfect,' I think. 'Everything is perfect!'

Dakk comes striding into the room with Ajay. Each of them carrying boxes of Drumsticks. The ice cream kind, not chicken legs, or the kind you actually use to play drums. Everyone cheers as they hold out their hands like children.

"Calm down, damn," Dakk says. He's grinning and trying to grab the tissue like plastic packages out of the boxes. He makes sure he gives Emma one first. Then we all take our seats, ice cream clutched in our hands, smiles across our faces. The third movie takes us on a journey to discover how to harness the power of 'Chi,' which is the energy that flows through all living things. Po's told that mastery of 'Chi' requires mastery over self.

The first, 'oh shit!' moment happens when Po's biological dad shows up at his adoptive fathers' restaurant. Po's excited to finally be around someone who looks like him. I know this thrill all too well. His adoptive father struggles over the idea of losing Po, so he decides to journey with the two pandas to their 'Secret Panda Village,' where Po believes he'll learn how to harness 'Chi.' The panda village is revealed through a vail of dispersing puffy white clouds. Po explodes with joy at the idea of finally finding where he belongs. There are so many inherent traits he shares with all these people. Yet, he also finds he struggles to learn and adapt to some of their ways.

During a scene where Po's panda dad was telling him the story of the attack, Dr. Cho comes up behind the couch and asks Brella to come with her for a moment. Emma and I both look over and see Brella nod her head before rising and heading toward the door. I can barely hear the door click shut after them because Po's just found out that his dad lied to him about being able to teach him how to harness, 'Chi.' Po feels betrayed and doesn't feel as though he can trust his dad again.

Po's dad and adoptive father have a heart to heart. Where the adoptive father confesses that he was afraid of losing Po to him. But now says, "I realize having you in Po's life didn't mean less for me. It means more for Po." Insert tears here. He goes on to explain that kids can be difficult and that as parents, "sometimes we do the wrong things for the right reasons." He concludes by adding, "He's hurt, he's confused, and he still has to save the world. He needs both his dads."

Together, Po, his dads, and his community of pandas work hard to learn Kung Fu in preparation for the attack on their village by Kai, stealer of 'Chi.' So, basically a dirty murderer. The final battle takes Po into the spirit realm, where he can safely fight Kai without the threat of anyone else being harmed. Po is nearly defeated when everyone in the village summons the power of 'Chi,' through summarizing the purpose Po has given to their lives and who they have discovered they are because of him. They join their life forces with his as the score crescendos.

I'm smiling big, watching Emma's face glowing in the light of the screen. Her eyes wide and glossy from tears. She's clutching her clasped hands to her chest before she rolls back, raising both arms in the air to cheers that fill the room. Po has turned Kai to dust.

When I first decided to show these movies for Emma's party, I wanted her to see someone else's journey. The disadvantage Po experienced because he wasn't meant to thrive in an environment that wasn't meant for him. The constant voice inside him that called him to a greater purpose despite being constantly put down, showing us not to give up. The power he found inside, the more he accepted himself along the way. His road wasn't easy, but in following it, he was able to become the warrior he was destined to be. And my only hope is that she understands the message behind this story.

Watching it again now, I realize it also taught me something new. Po didn't do all of this alone. He had so many people who were there for him. The family he found in Oogway, Shifu, and the Furious-Five. The identity he found in his biological dad and everyone in the panda village. His adoptive father, the goose, was able to fully accept and support Po as he went on this journey *with* him. So, I can finally see all these goofballs around me here; all the people I've known throughout my life, my family and friends back home, as well as all the people I'm yet to meet; are all a part of me. And I, a part of them. And it takes all of this together to know who I am.

Chollima

The sun was just beginning to set. Orange and pink, around the glowing golden sliver of an orb, still fighting to peak over the horizon. Emma was packing as I sat on my bed, watching through the window as the last rays slide away. Tomorrow the taxi would be here at 4:00 am to get her to the airport. And her flight will be taking off, just as the sun is waking on a new day.

'Please let it be sunny tomorrow,' I think, almost as though I'm saying a prayer.

Emma's movements are slow and composed. Her face doesn't reveal any sense of nervousness she may be feeling. So, I sit back on the bed, propping myself against the headboard and drawing my knees up to my chest, wrapping my arms around them. I watch Emma questioningly. And as though sensing my gaze, she looks up at me and gives me a reassuring smile before saying.

"Don't look so sad. I'm the one leaving."

"I know, but it's going to be so weird without you. It's just going to be me in here. All alone."

"No," she laughs. "You'll be alone for like a day before someone else comes in here. I just didn't have a suitemate sooner because I requested not to have one for the first week. I was shy, ya know?"

"Wait, you can request that?" I ask, arms hanging outstretched in a confused pose.

Emma laughs. "Yeah, you should know you can honestly request anything you want here because they're always supportive of our mental health."

"Anything?" I tease. "So, you're saying I'll have a new suitemate within days? That'll be weird. I'm just used to you. I connect with you."

"Well, who's to say you won't connect to this new person too? And isn't that the whole point? Creating relationships, not saying, I've created a relationship, so now I'm done. But continuing to create relationships."

She strides over to me now. Her face is serious but gentle at the same time. And she sits, one knee resting on the mattress. Reaching out her hand, she pulls one arm loose from clutching my legs and says, "I'm going to miss you too, Van, so much. You have no idea how scared I am to leave. But I'm not going to let those feelings of fear and uncertainty hold me back anymore. And you aren't either. You promise me? Promise me, Van!" Her tiny face is fierce, and it makes me break the pitiful expression I'd been holding on my face.

I laugh and fold my legs criss-cross under me before leaning in, embracing her. I have my face smashed into her hair against her shoulder. It's extremely awkward and uncomfortable, but I bear it for a moment before letting go. I lean back against the headboard again.

"I promise," I say.

"And you aren't going to get super bummed out and

waste time throwing a pity party for yourself after I leave, are you? Because you only have so much time to get the most out of everything here, Van."

"I know, I know! I laugh to Emma. I promise, promise you, that I will not stop for anything!" I'm holding my hands out, fingers pressed together, palm to palm.

And fat tears fall from her eyes at this. She was too tired to hold back the sadness anymore. Her fears were extinguished, and she felt assured I would be okay now. She could stop being strong for me.

"I'm seriously going to miss you so much. Call me as soon as you leave here, and we'll make a plan to meet up some weekend. Okay?" she questions.

"Okay, I promise I will, as soon as I leave here," I say.

Ashes

I tried not to fall asleep. I wanted to get up and walk Emma to the door. Watch the taillights of her Uber disappear into the black of the night. But instead, I'm being roused by a cheerful voice in the doorway, letting me know it was time to begin my day.

I look up to the yellow beams streaming in from under the blinds. And smile, forgiving myself a little, at least Emma took off into the sky just as the sun was rising.

'That would have made her happy,' I think, bouncing myself up from the bed.

Breakfast is just starting to be served when I reached the cafeteria. I don't want to wait in line, so I go sit at our usual table. It's empty at the moment, and I'm glad to be able to sit here alone. Time to prepare myself for the moments to follow when the tables will be full, except for where Emma would be. I close my eyes and do deep breathing techniques for a minute or so before Moon's voice interrupts.

"Deep cleansing breath in...and ouuuuuuuut."

"Uuuuuuuugh," I say, resting my face down against the table.

"Dude, look, get up, eat something. It's sunny. We can hang out outside all day if you want," he encourages.

"When do you leeeeeave?" I joke.

"Whenever I want. I keep extending my days, and they keep letting me stay," he snorts. "I like it here," and yanks me up by my arm.

Just as we're getting to the end of the line for bagels, doughnuts, and different types of croissants, Dr. Cho rushes up to me. Her eyes are urgent, and it startles me. She's trying to put on the façade that she's composed, but her panting breath is giving her away.

"Van, please come with me – Moon, it's okay. I'll speak with you later. Or your therapist will speak with you later. Van, please." She's holding her arm out in the direction of her office, and I start walking mechanically. My heart is pounding so hard I can feel it beating against the flesh on my back. There are 14,000,605 ways something terrible has happened.

'Please, please let this be the reality where everything will turn out okay,' I'm thinking to myself, over and over, until we get to Dr. Cho's office.

She flips on the light, and I realize this must be the first time she's been in her office this morning. I look harder at her face now, focusing on her tired, slightly sunken eyes, the tight look of her mouth as she fumbles to place her jacket on the back of her desk chair. The messiness of her hair. And she's wearing the same clothes she'd had on yesterday.

There's a large rock sitting in my stomach. I'm standing hunched over, the heaviness of it makes it difficult not to topple over.

"Please just tell me what's going on," I finally force myself to gasp out after moments pass, arms wrapped tight around my stomach.

"Sorry, yes, sorry, Van, please, sit down," she says, shaking her head as though forcing herself out of a trance.

She takes a seat in her usual chair, and I sit nervously, hoovering on the edge of the couch.

"Van," her voice shakes. "Brella received a phone call last night." Dr. Cho's eyes, which normally remain fixed on my face, are lowered to the rug on the floor as though she's reading these words printed on it. "It was her sister, from China. She told Brella that their mother had been struck by a passing vehicle. It was such a complete freak accident, it could have happened to anyone," She was trailing, her eyes unfocused. "Van, her mother didn't survive."

I watch her eyes well up with tears, and she plucks a tissue from the box on the end table, pressing it to her face before the tears can fall.

"Where's Brella?" I ask. Knowing she'll need me. That she'll need as much support as we can all give her.

"Van," Dr. Cho's voice is barely a whisper. "Brella's gone."

"What do you mean gone?" I demand. "You let her leave? She would have been out of her mind from grief, and you just let her walk out the door? Did she leave on foot, or did someone pick her up?"

"Van!"

"Did anyone try to stop her?"

"Van!" Dr. Cho snaps.

And I let the hard expression on my face melt when I watch her deflate in front of me. She sits back hard in the chair, her slumping body looks completely deflated before her hand reaches up to cover her eyes.

"Brella's dead, Van. I'm so sorry." These words were sent on breaths, deep sorrowful pants escaping from her.

I feel the resonating thud in my chest the moment my

heart stops. It's worse than Dr. Strange predicted. This was worse than Tony's death in End Game. This was real. There's a ringing in my ears—low distorted ringing. It drowns out every word that comes out of Dr. Cho's mouth afterward. I just stop processing everything. The screen in front of my eyes freezes then goes to a blurry snowy gray fuzz. I don't feel anything. I don't exist anywhere. Everything has stopped. Everything fades to black.

Float

Jayden
Day 24
~~I'm sorry~~   ~~I wasn't~~

***

Day 25
~~I'm so sorry~~

***

Day 26

***

Day 27
Jayden

It's Moon – I'm here

***

I'm woken by a crunching warm croissant being smashed against my closed mouth. I move my face away, but the buttery pastry is crushed against the general area of my face where my lips are again, leaving flaky crumbs and grease smears. I raise my arms and use one to shield my face from another attack while the other flails around, trying to fight off this aggressive force feeder.

"Stahp," I groan.

"You have to eat something," he says, voice determined as he tries to force his restrained arm close enough to reach my mouth.

The croissant is smashed between his fingers, flatter than a pancake, but he's still persistent. I look up into his face as crumbs fall on me, and I can't help it. I just start laughing. As soon as the sound bursts out of me, Moon's eyebrows raise. His expression is relaxed now, and his face reflects his relief as he shouts.

"She's alive!" Before laughing hysterically with his head thrown back, mimicking the mad Dr. Frankenstein in the old black and white film. He's standing on his knees on my bed, and I pull my pillow out from behind my head, smashing it against his face to get him to shut up.

He topples onto the mattress, springing me up in the process, before laughing and sitting up against my headboard. I pull myself up, too, so we're sitting side by side. Looking at the vacant space Emma used to fill.

"I wish she was here," I say quietly, looking down now. "But I'm also, you know, glad she wasn't here for this."

"Are you going to tell her?" he asks, still looking forward.

"Yeah, I'll tell her. But not until after I leave. I just can't do it right now," I explain though I know it's not necessary.

Moon tries to hand me the demolished piece of breakfast food again, and I smile and nudge his shoulder with mine, shaking my head with a grossed-out expression.

"You want to go get some fresh food?" he suggests. "I haven't eaten yet."

I give him a knowing look because it's obvious he's lying. He wouldn't have gone to the cafeteria to grab this for me without shoveling something in his mouth along the way. But I start getting up anyway.

I use the bathroom first, and as I flip the switch on to the low humming of the light above the sink, I breathe in the air, still full of Emma's strawberry-scented shampoo. It's as though she's just been here and will be waiting for me outside the door. And I close my eyes and soak in the smell for a moment longer before looking at myself in the mirror.

My face is puffy and sunken at the same time. My eyes aren't even their normal shape—they're so swollen. I run cold water and let it run over my fingers. Then I cup my hands together and let them fill before placing my eyes into the shallow pool. The chill of it awakening my entire body with goosebumps. I do this several more times until I can see that some of the swelling has gone down.

I come out as I'm pulling my hair up into a ponytail. Moon is scribbling something in my journal and doesn't notice me until I pull the bathroom door shut, letting it slam behind me. He jumps then hurriedly finishes what he's writing before springing from my bed.

Walking down the white hall feels like being in a dream. My body moves sluggishly, and I'm debating going back to my room. But the more we walk, I'm starting to hear the low rumbling of voices along with the clattering of silverware. I can smell the sweet scents of pastries as we near mixed with the spices of baked beans and strong sausages. My stomach is letting me know how angry it is that I haven't fed it for days. I clutch my abdomen to try to calm the loud grumbling roars escaping from it. I first grab a half stack of pancakes, then dish up some scrambled eggs and fork two small sausage patties on top. I get to the hash browns and pile them on, too, before covering everything in creamy white country gravy.

As I get to the table, I pause, taking in the emptiness. It's just Moon and Ajay. Everyone else is gone. I lower my eyes to the food on my tray that I no longer have an appetite for. But my attention is drawn back as I hear the familiar sound of chair legs scraping on the tile floor. Dakk's lowering himself to slump in the chair. Just then, Sunni and Kate scamper up, teasingly fighting for the chair next to him. Raafe saunters up and timidly asks if he can sit with us. He looks exhausted. And I nod before setting my tray on the table and taking my usual seat. I pan around to look at everyone's faces. They're all smiling and chatting. Moon dunks a piece of toast into the fountain of gravy on my plate while laughing at something Ajay just said. None of them realizing what they had just done. My heart is beating again. I can feel the heavy pounding in my chest, each pump inflating it like a balloon that swells inside me.

I fork a little bit of everything on my plate and shove it in my mouth. My eyes involuntarily close as I chew the warm, sweet, salty, peppery, creamy concoction in my mouth. When I open them, I see everyone's eyes on me.

"Waa?" is all I can get out around all the food.

"After you finish," Moon says quietly, "we should all go smoke."

I nod and finish about a fourth of my plate before I can't eat anymore. Your stomach shrinks a lot when you aren't stretching it out every day.

As we reach the smoking sign, Dakk lights up a joint. As it

THE ONES WHO MISBEHAVE

passes from my hand to Raafe's, his trembling fingers give him away before he collapses onto the bench. His face is in his hands, and he's sobbing. Kate sits beside him now, hugging him tightly. I look to Moon in my confusion.

"Raafe found Brella," he leans in and whispers to me.

I rush up to Raafe, the knees of my jeans skidding into the ground at his feet. I don't know if I'm asking him to tell me what happened because I'm looking for answers. More because not knowing hasn't made me feel any better so far.

Sunni pulls a tissue from her tiny crossbody and hands it to him. He blows his nose and starts at the beginning.

"I'd gone to the pharmacy because I hadn't slept well for several nights, and I was starting to feel a little, 'off,' so I decided to see if they could give me something. Just to help me stay asleep," he wipes his eyes quickly before continuing. "I didn't see anybody at the desk when I got to the floor, and that was the first weird thing. So, I kinda yelled, like calling out to see if anyone was there."

"Was anyone there?" I ask.

He shakes his head no before going on. "I walked up to the door of the pharmacy and kinda looked around. But I didn't see anyone. I know the general area where the sleeping aids are kept, so I just walked in. That's when I heard a sound coming from...somewhere. It scared me, is all I know. So, I kinda paced up and down the hall where the offices are, and I heard a sort of shuffling sound inside Dr. Cody's office. I knocked on the door cause I was really hoping there was someone around who could help me. Then I heard the crash inside, and I just opened the door," he closes his eyes and shakes his head as if trying to erase the memory like an etch-a-sketch board. "And it was Brella. She was having some sort of seizure or something. There were all these pills around her on the floor, and she was flopping around, but like, stiff. Like a fish out of water," he stops and

121

squeezes the bridge of his nose between his fingers. "I ran over to her and tried to hold her head and some of the things I've seen people do on tv, but she was like foaming at the mouth or something. I got scared, and I went to get help," his shoulders are shaking as he tries to contain his emotions enough to finish. "But when we got back, she was gone, Van." He crumbles into Kate's shoulder.

I'm looking around, searching everyone's faces for clues that there's more to it as tears tumble down my cheeks. I meet Moon's eyes, and he jerks his head, indicating I should come talk to him. I rest my hand on Raafe's knee tenderly as I raise myself off the ground.

Moon and I are standing a little way back from the group. He tells me that Brella had gotten super sad after hearing about her mom. He said she had a note in her pocket when they found her.

"It said, 'I just want to be with my family. I'm sorry, I can't wait anymore.'"

I close my eyes and can feel the tears burst free from between my eyelashes. I have my hands clasped closed together, pressed hard against my forehead, almost as though I'm about to pray. But instead, I scream. Not a scream of terror. The kind of scream that happens when you have no other way to express the feelings inside of you. The kind of sound that comes from the deepest depths of yourself. The place you push all your anger. Your sadness, humiliation, despair, anguish, loneliness, confusion, grief, disappointment. Until it all comes rushing out of you as a loud, tormented cry. An animal sound you didn't know could come out of you.

"We could have been her family," I say more to myself than out loud.

And then all I know is I'm being crushed by bodies and limbs from everyone around me. Holding me up. Holding me together. I see Raafe's sullen face and pull him to me, and his slender body shakes against me with sobs. We all cry together. Some silently, some can't contain the sounds that emerge from them. And we share a moment of absolute mourning as a tribe under the California sun. We honor our friend, who can now be at peace. And birds sing, and the breeze blows. And I turn my face up to the sky.

"Brella," I say in a breath.

Toast

We stayed outside all day. Soaking in the rays of the sun while lounging on the grass. Eating our lunch and dinner picnic-style on the ground. Even though we all knew we could skip our classes and sessions, it still felt a little bit like we were ditching high school to go smoke under the bleachers.

Moon's legs are straight out in front of him as he rests back, propped up on his elbows. I'm laying on my stomach with my arms folded under my chin, my eyes closed.

"You know," he says pensively, "I've never had any of the issues some of the people here have."

"What do you mean?" I ask, even though I know what he means. I just couldn't think of anything else to say.

"I mean, some people here have had it super rough. You know, abuse, neglect...sexual...stuff," he whispers the last words leaning over like it's a secret.

"Who cares!" I say, copying a response he'd once given

me. We both smile at the reminiscence. "Dude, look," I start, squinting against the sun to look up at him. "It doesn't matter. It's not a competition. No one here is keeping a chart of who had the most trauma growing up. Your shit is your shit, and yours isn't less just because someone else's is more." I smile to myself for remembering how Dr. Cho had once guided me through these feelings.

He snorts, "I won't argue with that. But I can't stop being angry about it, like all the time. It's this rage inside me for everyone who suffers, and it turns to anger and resentment, and guilt. Like what made my life so unbearable that I keep coming back here? I was given a good life. I was supported…financially anyway. So, I have gratitude for that. Their monetary contribution to my future and well-being. But at what point do I stop feeling owned. I mean, I was purchased. I was a product—an exotic designer baby. And like Brella told us, a plaything for her parent's real children. A way to make sure they got a girl and not another boy. A product." His face is sour. I can feel his sadness and the hurt inside him radiating. "We shouldn't have to suffer because of their ignorance. Do they think we can't feel it? What we really are? They change our names to fit their American households, like Hanna or Josh. Giving us a fighting chance to get a real job because we have names that are easier to pronounce - Americanized. There are pieces of me that are stolen. And no one's ever apologized to me for that. I'm not a fucking dog who's just so happy to be alive and fed and sheltered and shit. And then completely off-topic, but what the fuck is up with people tagging their pets as adoptees? Hashtag Adoptee, hashtag that's insulting to fucking actual human adoptees." His eyes are wild, but hints of laughter are shining through, and I can tell he's back from the internal place he'd barely dipped his toe into.

But I'm laughing because he's so right! And I roll over

onto my back and hold my stomach, dying from this giggle fit.

"What the hell are ya'll laughing about?" Dakk calls over.

I sit up now, wiping the tears that were rolling out of my eyes. "Oh my God," I pant, "Moon was seriously just saying that he hates it when people tag their pets as adoptees on social media."

Everyone bursts into laughter.

"Aaaaaaahhhhhh! That's hilarious and true. Never thought about it before, but shit's kinda fucked up though, for real," Dakk says.

"On that note, it's time to go in, guys," Sunni chimes in, standing up and stretching her back, arms raised over her head.

I get up and do the same. Feeling my body waking up from its repose. We collect all the trash we've littered the space with and take turns shooting our crumpled wads of garbage into the metal bins as we near the center. We all say our goodnights and give each other long hugs before retreating to our suites.

After a long hot shower, I jump into bed and grab Jayden. I'm just opening my journal as I hear a gentle knock at the open-door frame.

"Hi," I say politely to the guide standing there, not getting up.

She says, "Dr. Cho would like to request a session tomorrow morning at 7:30. Are you comfortable speaking with her, or do you think you still need some time?"

I smile at her warmly, "Please tell her I'll be there. 7:30 sharp."

The girl nods at me, then turns and goes, pulling the open door shut behind her. I open Jayden again and am trying to find the last filled page. As I turn them, I click my pen in preparation but stop when I get to the page Moon had been scratching on this morning. I forgot all about that, and I smile to myself as I read the quote I recognize from The Secret Life of Walter Mitty: "To see the world, things dangerous to come to, to see behind walls, to draw closer, to find each other and to feel. That is the purpose of life."

Pulling the book to my chest, I cradle it in my arms. Tears begin to fall as I smile and fall back into my pillow. Holding my journal open above my face, I click the pen.

***

Jayden

Day 27 has been a really good day. It's time to get off my ass tomorrow!

***

Gwishin

Gently knocking with the very tips of my knuckles, I hear Dr. Cho's voice from inside calling me to come in. The room is glowing warm with morning sunshine. I give a small smile as I pass her desk to go sit in my chair.

She's been watching me carefully since I walked through the door. Her mouth breaks into a gentle grin at my slight gesture of assurance. She stands and walks over to me, stretching out her arms. I stand up and give her a warm embrace.

"Ooooooh," she grunts mid-squeeze and starts rubbing my back like she's trying to warm me up before finally releasing me. "I'm not going to ask how you are. That's a ridiculous question to start with after everything," she asserts.

Giggling a little, I reply, "Okay, good. I'm getting tired of that one anyway."

"I'm just glad to see you. I was so happy to see you out of

your room yesterday. That was a huge step. We weren't going to push you to participate, and you know you can stay as long as you like. If you want to stay longer, you know we would welcome the extension."

I stare at her for a moment, not sure if I've made a decision about that yet, before finally replying, "I've been considering it. I know Moon says he's extended his stay. But I made a promise to Emma that I would be out a week after her and we would get together as soon as I left here. I mean, I told her I would call her as soon as I was on my way to the airport...so..." I was staring out the window as I said this but turn to look firmly at Dr. Cho as I say, "I want to keep my promise."

"Good," she smiles. "That sounds like a great plan." She pauses before asking, "Emma doesn't know about Brella yet, does she?"

"I'm going to tell her. I've decided I'm going to tell her in person. I can't stand the idea of her dealing with everything alone. She won't survive it," I confess, with a worried glance at Dr. Cho.

"Everybody processes things differently," she encourages. "Everybody grieves differently, Van. Emma is fragile, but she's also strong. You were here when you were told about Brella. You weren't alone, but you needed time alone for a while to heal in your own way before opening yourself back up to people."

"I get what you're saying," I reply, "but I," I say, pressing my hand to my chest, "I need to be there for her. *I* need that for me to feel okay."

Dr. Cho smiles at me comfortingly. "And once you know Emma's okay, only then will you feel okay too?"

I'm getting confused. I'm feeling trapped. I'm trying to regain composure when I just let it all come out.

"I'll never feel okay!" I say, curling up in the chair, knees against my chest, face in hands. "I don't understand why she did it! I mean, I do," I squeak through my tears, "but I...I'm just so mad! At everything and everyone. Why was no one there to stop her? Why did Raafe say no one was at the desk? Someone should have been there! Someone should have been there to stop her!" I'm screaming now, leaned so far forward I would fall out of the chair if I wasn't gripping the arms hard enough to crush them. "Brella's dead! Brella's dead, and Raafe will be fucked up for the rest of his life. And it didn't have to be this way! So, someone, please explain to me why! Why does this shit keep happening?"

Dr. Cho pulls a tissue from the box and holds it out to me. I let my grip loosen and reach to take it.

"Van, I wish I could tell you exactly what you need to know. To have the words that will give you comfort and a sense of serenity. But I don't. No one will. There aren't ever going to be answers that will be good enough because there are too many questions. The only thing I can say with absolute certainty is – you gave Brella so much love, Van. And no one knows when we will lose those that we choose to love. It's always going to hurt. No matter how we lose someone. But while she was with you, she was loved."

"But it wasn't enough," I say weakly.

"It was everything," Dr. Cho assures me, eyes wide and glossy and filled with hope. She stands up and walks over to sit on the sofa beside my chair. Her thin fingers reach out to rest on my knee. It's warm. A gesture of understanding. A physical connection. I slowly slide my hand under hers, and she curls her fingers and squeezes.

And we sit, hand in hand, a scared child, a comforting mother.

Ellipsis

Before leaving Dr. Cho's office, she hands me a slip of paper with a picture and a description. As I lift my eyes questioning, she tells me that this is my new suitemate who's arriving in an hour.

"Look for her at lunch, Van. She'll need someone to help her adjust," she squeezes my shoulder as she guides me to the door and says, "You're ready."

"But I'm only here for two more days," I mention, a bit thrown off by this information.

"Don't worry, I think that'll be plenty of time," she smiles. "Do you know what you want to do to celebrate your last day?"

I hesitate, thinking, "I don't really want to do anything. We just did something for Emma, and with everything, I just want everything to be normal until I go. Plus, I didn't graduate, so a party would be pretty wasted on me. But I'll talk to you on my last day, right?"

"Yes, same time as today," she says, going to her

computer and leaning down to scroll before continuing. "You know, you could graduate, Van. You just need to complete four more groups."

"Four? So, if I could get to three tomorrow and then one my last day, I could graduate?" I say, the idea lighting my face. Emma will be so happy. "Okay, I smile at Dr. Cho. I accept the challenge."

"I knew you would," she chimes. "Now, do you want to celebrate?"

"Nah," I shrug, heading toward the doorway. "I'll celebrate with Emma when I G.T.F.O!!!"

I go back to my suite. I'm not hungry, and I want to get all Dr. Cho's books together, so I remember to take them with me to my last appointment. As I'm dusting the covers with a towel, I hear footsteps moving fast down the hall, and I turn just in time to see Moon and Dakk come rushing in. They're gasping air and laughing. Moon tries to catch his breath before spewing out what just happened.

"Oh my God! Dude!" he's saying in pants. "The new girl just got into it out there!" he laughs, holding his stomach.

"She straight up punched this chick in the side of her head out there!" Dakk spouts. "Then they pulled her away kickin' and shit."

I'm staring at them with my mouth hanging open, which quickly transforms into a full-face grin.

"I can't wait to meet her," I say. "I think that's my new suitemate."

"Awwww shit, here we go with these crazy Asians," Dakk jokes.

"I bet they took her to Dr. Cho's office. She's Korean," I say, holding up the little slip of paper that I pulled from my pocket. "And she's adopted," I giggle.

Moon's eyes light up, and he nudges his head toward the door. And we all take off, shoving each other to get through the door first. All you could hear in the hallway was the sound of our shoes squeaking against the tiles among the echoes of our laughter until we reached Dr. Cho's door. Cupping our hands over our mouths, we try to stifle the sounds of our heavy breathing. Each of us finds a spot to press our ears against the wood, but we found that wasn't necessary. A raging voice of fluctuating muffled words slowly grows louder. I start moving back with the realization this person was headed right toward the door. I pull Dakk and Moon by their shirt collars just in time to miss this person who'd passed us so quickly she was a blur. All I could see was her long dark hair swinging agitatedly back and forth as she strode quickly away from us.

Moon taps our elbows as he passes us, "I know where she's going. Follow me."

I smile knowingly to myself as we head toward the double doors.

Chit Chat

As we approach the smoking sign, this little cloud of ferocious gloom turns to face us. She's wearing black calf high lace-up army boots. Dark gray jeans and an oversized black t-shirt with bright yellow letters that read, 'Wu-Tang,' across the front peeking out from behind her folded arms. She's shorter than me by several inches, and thicker than me around her ass and thighs.

'*Way* sturdier than Emma,' I think to myself.

I raise my hand up and let Moon and Dakk know I was going to talk to her by myself for a second. Their shoulders relax a little, and they turn to go, but hover close by.

"Where are you from?" I say, approaching cautiously.

"Fuck off!" she replies.

Ignoring her response, I continue as though she answered me. "No, but where are you from, originally?" I chime, raising my eyebrows a little to indicate I was waiting for her to catch on to what I was doing. This standard but rude series of questions is something we receive on a regular basis by ignorant people who don't seem to realize how intrusive it is.

I catch the slight change in her hard expression. The break that shows me she's now more curious about me than angry by my presence. She still hasn't replied, but I continue, "Do you plan to go back to your home country?" I crack a smile at this but keep going. I know she's caught on to what I'm doing. "I know this guy who has an Asian wife." She's staring at me, so I go on, "I knew a lot of good Koreans back in the war," I begin but am interrupted by the sounds of laughter breaking out of the girl's pressed lips.

And I look at her and start cracking up.

"I'm May," she says, still giggling.

"I'm Van, Vanessa, but I go by Van," I reply. "I just want to tell you, May," I smirk, "You speak English really well."

And we both burst with laughter, tears being squeezed out from the corners of our eyes.

"Alright, I'm done," I say. "I'm your suitemate. Or will be until I leave in two days."

"Cool, then what, I'll get a new person after you leave?" she asks.

"Yeah, but you might have a day or two without one."

"That's fine. I'm not for everyone if you know what I mean," she shrugs.

"I definitely know exactly what you mean," I reply.

I pull out a joint and light it up before taking a seat on the bench. May follows suit as I hold it out to her.

"They let you smoke weed here?" she talks a while holding in her drawn breath.

"They give it to you here!" I explain.

Her eyes widen, and she smiles as she exhales loudly, "Maybe I am going to like it here."

After a few passes back and forth in silence, I ask with a

grin, "So where are you from, seriously this time."

"Alabama," she giggles.

"Kansas," I point at myself, "So basically the only other Asian people you see work at the nail salon or restaurants, right?"

"Pretty much, yeah," she huffs.

"It sucks," I shrug, "I know how weird that is. And it always made me feel guilty, like, it took growing up and going to get my nails done to wake up and realize I was ridiculously privileged." I tilt my head forward to try to read her expression. "And it just showed me I was different. That I wasn't part of this community of people either. They would all chat with each other in their language. And I looked like these people who couldn't relate to me at all, and it was like I didn't even exist, just a white Asian girl."

May turns to look at me now. Her eyes are warm, and she says, "I know exactly what you mean. So, you're adopted too?"

"Yep, there's a bunch of us here," I explain, nodding in Moon's direction. "That's Moon. He's a Korean adoptee too. With trauma, just like the rest of us. When I came here, I attacked the other guy, Dakk, but we're cool now. We're not so different, you and I."

After a long pause, she asks, "And you're better now?"

"I am," I answer, doing a quick scroll through the filmstrip of my memories made during my time here. "When I got here, I was pissed off at everyone and everything. But after all this, I feel really okay with myself, ya know?" I say, smiling and leaning my head back to feel the sun on my face.

Moon and Dakk are making their way over. I guess they decided it was safe. I make introductions before saying I was going to grab a drink inside really quick.

I make a detour to my suite and flop onto my stomach when I get to my bed. I lay for a minute or two, enjoying the calm and silence.

Then I reach over and grab Jayden, opening to the next blank page.

***

Jayden
New roomies here! She and I are going to get along just fine.

Her name is May! She's the new me!
Day 28 – where the hell did time go?

***

Slow Burn

May and I grab our dinners to go. Her panic-attack standing in line was pretty epic, so I just grabbed her elbow and pulled her to the sandwiches. I tried to do a quick tour as we went.

"That's the Italian station, great pizza – This is Cantonese, Japanese, awesome sushi, Indian, Mediterranean, amazing spinach pies."

We snatch up Cheetos and sodas, and she seems to be calming down a little since getting out of the crowded line. I can hear my name being called. I don't have to turn around to know it's Moon. I give May a light nudge with my elbow and nod in the direction of our hallway. As we rush forward, I look over and mouth to Moon, 'going to room, sorry.' He nods back and sits down, looking bummed out.

Shuffling into our suite with loot in tow, I rush over to set my soda on my nightstand. As I'm setting the rest down on my bed, I nod over to the empty side of the room.

"That's all you," I say, giving her a reassuring smile.

"Where's my stuff?" She asks.

"What?" I puzzle, walking over to look around. Her suitcase was not sitting patiently next to her bed like mine had been. "Well, shit! Um, let's eat, and then when we go to dump our trash in the cafeteria after everyone else is out of there, we can ask the people at the guest counter."

"Okay," she smiles and gently dumps the items out of her arms onto the bed.

We eat hurriedly, not engaging in any real conversation. I could tell May was growing extremely anxious, and I wanted us to get answers as soon as possible. We collect all the trash and head toward the main entrance. I tell May to go ahead, and I would throw everything away and catch up to her. She nods and heads off.

As I'm approaching the front desk, I can hear May before I see her. She's screaming, not yelling, screaming at the top of her lungs. My pace increases, and I begin to sprint until I reach May. Her face is red, eyes filled with wild rage, and she's panting as though she's breathing fire.

"Where's May's luggage?" I ask a blonde Australian man, standing behind the desk, who politely replies.

"Another resident volunteeyad to take it to her room for 'a, all I know dahling, awful sorry for the mix-up."

May's pacing, soon there will be a track on the floor where she's been circling. Arms folded tight around her stomach. Tears trickle out of her eyes, and she wipes at them quickly.

"What resident?" I ask through clenched teeth.

His blonde head bobs around, seeing if he can spot her in the courtyard before locking his eyes and pointing, "Thah."

My eyes follow his finger, and I see her. It was the girl Dakk had pointed to earlier when he told me about May punching her in the head.

I don't even glance at her as I stride toward the double doors. As I'm approaching, I can see that shit's about to get much worse. I could see a tornado had hit May's suitcase and scattered all of her belongings around. A tornado called – Kalifa. The very same that had told me to, 'Go back to my country.'

I stop as soon as I step foot outside. The mess was enormous. T-shirts, jeans, underwear – strung up in trees. Other articles of clothing sat in lumps on the ground or draped over the mouths of trash cans. Bathroom items dabble the grass, a bar of deodorant by my feet. Toothpaste here, shampoo over there. My gaze moving from this item to the next in disbelief.

I'm shoved forward as May forces her way through the door. Mouth gaping in horror. Turning her head, slowly taking in the sight of all her personal belongings, the way you'd stand and watch a tidal wave coming straight for you.

"What in the actual fuck, Kalifa!" I scream.

Kalifa snaps up, and she freezes. May just stands there, staring until tears pop from her bottom eyelids and drip down her cheeks.

Several security members and guides rush out. Two of the guides, the Australian and a short Latina woman, go over to Kalifa and start herding her inside. Others tell May they'll collect her things, apologizing fiercely, but I can see in her eyes that she's already gone. Withdrawn inside herself so much, their voices don't reach her. I try to look into her eyes. I turn her face to me, and I speak quickly, trying to be optimistic. But her eyes are glazed over, she's unresponsive, and I stand there as a security guard guides her back inside gently, one arm resting across her shoulder.

"Are they taking May to her therapist?" I ask, getting no answer at first. "Hey!" I say, striding up to the next person, "Where are they taking, May? Is Kalifa kicked out? She needs to be kicked out, like now!"

"Go back to your suite. I'm sure someone will give you answers soon."

I reluctantly return to my suite. What else can I do? Everything is a mess. I let the door slam behind me and fall back on my bed. Sighing loudly.

I lay here and wait as minutes pass. I strain my eyes for the sounds of any movement in the hall, sometimes catching myself holding my breath. My fingers start getting jittery, and I decide I need to do something instead of just sit here waiting. I reach for Jayden and click my pen.

***

Jayden

***

I tap the pen against the page. Trying to think of how to start. I just start scribbling and trust something will come to mind.

***

Fucking Kalifa, man, how is she not gone already after the shit she pulled her first day with me. And now she threw May's shit all over the courtyard. Like everything, everywhere! I would be so pissed. I am pissed! And May punched her in the head earlier, but this time she just like froze up. Or gave up. I assume she's with her therapist now, but I have no idea. I'm waiting for someone to come to tell me something.

It really fucking sucks that some people hate Asians because they think we're like, super successful and have it really easy or something. Like we're not a threat to white people, so we are tolerated by them more. But that's not true.

I wish there was no such thing as hate. I wish we didn't feel the need to compare ourselves to others and be angry about what we believe someone else has. There's so much anger, and I get it. Things have been fucked up way too long, and we're living in a cycle. I can't imagine what it would feel like to be asleep in your bedroom one minute and shot and killed the next. I can't pretend to know the terror that goes through a black man's heart when he's pulled over by the police when he didn't do anything wrong. I'm privileged to not know what living like that feels like. And I know this. But that doesn't mean I don't feel the pain of their loss, all those countless lives taken without any reason. I don't know why I feel it so deeply. But it tears me apart inside to watch names pop up on a screen telling me another person of color was killed or tortured, raped, stabbed, beaten, set on fire. And know that millions will scroll past without even caring to learn this person's story.

That name is a life.

So, I understand being angry. Because I am so angry. But I refuse to hate! No matter what our differences may be, no matter if I know you or not, I will not be controlled by hate.

However, that does not mean I won't tell your stupid ass off when you say some dumb racist shit to me!

Van

***

Hibachi

I hadn't heard anything about May until the following day. The salt and pepper haired leader in my first group had slipped me a note that Dr. Cho had asked him to give me. It was quick and simple, 'May decided to leave. I'm sorry I didn't touch base with you last night. Come talk if you need to.' I folded the paper and shoved it deep inside my pocket. I wasn't upset she decided to leave. I just felt sad for her. That her experience here had been bad. That, that bitch, Kalifa, wasn't kicked out a long time ago. That she wouldn't be able to see how amazing everyone she would have been around could be. How they could change her life. But I was also glad that she got away because I was thinking of Brella now and how I would have rather her have left that night. I'd rather she'd done anything else. So, I wish May peace in her life and let it go.

The next two groups had gone by in a sort of blur. I watched everyone's faces more closely. Memorizing their eyes and their expressions. Knowing that it was all coming to an end made everything bittersweet. I had to keep telling myself, 'You can always come back. And you will always have the friends you made here.'

I caught up with Moon at lunch, and we decided to spend the rest of the day going to an outdoor yoga class and then do something we've never tried before – Asian cooking class. We'd heard about it from Ajay, and he was told by Delphine.

We all mosey to the cafeteria area around 2:00 pm. There are ten people standing around, each looking around between light conversations. Ajay and Delphine walk up and stand beside us. Delphine's a tall, gorgeous Brazilian with rich bronze skin and shiny burnt caramel-colored hair. Her eyes are piercingly green, though she claims they're hazel. My face is almost touching hers as I lean in close, barely able to see the specs of brown right around her pupil, as a thick Asian accent breaks through the chatters.

The man is dressed in a white chef's coat with a tall red paper hat. He explains that he is the hibachi cook and will be teaching us how to make fried rice. We all look around at each other, smiles bursting on our faces.

The first thing we did was put on crisp white aprons and clear vinyl gloves. Then we paired up and stood in front of a hot deep stove top with large black woks at each station. We pour the oil in, and it explodes in a rage of fiery hisses. We laugh at each other every time we'd shake our woks, and it would begin spitting searing fireworks, exploding on our exposed skin.

First, we sprinkle in some prechopped green and yellow onion. As Moon shuffles the wok like a pro while holding his head far from his outstretched arm. I crack two eggs and watch the yellow yokes break and spread inside the whites. Next, Moon turns the bowl, holding the butter upside down, letting it fall into the steaming mixture.

"Holy shit! Were you supposed to put all that in there?" I ask frantically.

"I don't know! Let's just go with it!" he smiles.

I decide to just cover it up with rice, and I scoop a chunk of the heavy white rice up in my fingers before dropping it the wok.

"Fuck this!" I say, turning the bowl over and letting it all fall in, then scooping the remaining pieces out with my hand.

"You just gotta go for it." Moon encourages, dumping on the bowl of soy sauce, then sesame oil.

I revolve the bowl of salt and pepper as I pour it over the sizzling contents.

"Smells amazing," I say, breathing the steam in deep.

Moon's still shaking the wok, side to side, then pulling it forward before thrusting it back, causing the ingredients inside to swoop into the air and land back inside. We'd been given a wood spatula to stir with, but he hadn't touched it. We didn't notice why this would be a problem until we went to pour our fried rice into our bowls, and a giant chunk of egg fell out.

We both start cracking up and don't stop until tears are rolling down our faces and our stomachs cramp. Every time we attempt to try the product of our cooking, one of us would either burst out laughing or make choking noises trying to hold it in. It took about five minutes to calm down enough to take a bite. And it was worth it. Surprisingly, it tasted like really good Hibachi fried rice. I held my right arm up, not looking up from my bowl. Without skipping a beat, Moon's arm shoots up, and his hand collides with mine in a perfect high-five.

Ha na

As the golden pink rays of the awakening sun stretch their fingers beneath my blinds, I'm already awake and dressed. Hunter green suitcase packed and waiting patiently near the foot of my bed. I'm just collecting Dr. Cho's books into a neat stack in my arms when I hear the gentle knock. I rush over to open the door with a smile for the guide.

"I'm up, I'm just getting ready to head that way," I say without waiting for them to speak. They simply nod and then turn and stride to the next room across the hall.

Dr. Cho's door is open when I arrive, and I stride in.

"Hey, hey!"

"Van," she smiles big, walking from her desk to embrace me, crushing the books between us. "Last day! How are you feeling?"

"I'm feeling really good, like, amazing, actually. Thanks for letting me read these," I hold the stack out to her. She fumbles with them before her tiny fingers are able to cradle them by the spines.

"Go ahead and sit down," she nods at my corner chair as she begins to slip each of the books back into their designated spot among the clutter of her shelves.

I'm smiling to myself as I take a seat, remembering my first time in this room. I'm gazing around now, the same way I'd done then. Without a hint of nervousness or fear. Without feeling the need to rush through 14,000,605 alternate realities to try to prepare myself for the worst possible outcome. And it isn't because I'm sitting in this familiar room or here at the center. I realize that for the first time in a long time, I feel safe inside myself.

"I learned a lot about myself reading those books," I say, watching her slide in the last one onto the shelf. "There were times I was so angry reading them, but, in the end, after learning all of their stories for myself, I found a kind of peace. Ya know? Because - I'm not alone. There's something peaceful in not feeling alone anymore," I pause, thinking for a moment before continuing. "And yes, I'm angry about the adoption system, I'm angry about the blindness people have toward the real damage being caused. I'm angry that children are suffering because they're seen as products and not people. And no one considers the feelings of a product. Like cows being led to slaughter without any feeling except a tingle in their wallets by those benefiting from the profits. The list goes on and on. But being angry doesn't change things. It just holds you back from having the courage to ask yourself, what can I do to make things better? Anger is destructive - it destroys and tears everything good apart. But hope," I wave a finger, "now that's something you can build on."

Dr. Cho's smiling at me warmly with an amused expression but says nothing. I go on.

"I've made the decision to allow myself to exist. Exactly

the way I am. I don't want to hate myself for having a good life. I don't want to feel guilty for being fucked-up. And I don't want to continue to blame myself for all the things I can't change," my voice catches, but I continue. "And after everything, I don't want to live my life being angry at other people, just because they're satisfied remaining in their comfort bubble. Do I wish they were different? Sure, but they aren't, and it doesn't matter," I stop to take a breath. "I have reasons I could use as excuses to continue to be angry. But I don't want to be anymore. I look back at all the ways my parents have been there for me. They took me to every dance lesson, celebrated every birthday, attended every lame school play. And if I called them up and needed anything, I know they'd drop everything to be here for me, right now, without question. That doesn't erase the things they did wrong. It doesn't mend the breaks that have been made over the years. But if I stop and really think about everything, what person doesn't have a complex over their parents? Most people have worse relationships with their biological parents than I do with my adoptive ones. All relationships are complicated, and everyone wishes there were things they could change about someone. But instead, let's all just exist, as we are. And if who they are can't accept who I am and who I want to become, then they are the ones choosing to lose me," I swallow, knowing that I've already made peace with this possible outcome. "And I'm tired of pretending they did this to me. The system did this to me. They just wanted a child. Sure, they made mistakes, but all parents make mistakes. If I'm a mother someday, I will make mistake after mistake. But if I've learned anything, it's that you make the best decision you can at the time. All the parents who gave their children up for adoption made a decision that affected us too. But they believe it was the best decision to make when they had to make it. No one's life is perfect. Everyone has their issues, and if we keep blaming everyone else, it'll never end," I pause. "My family's lives are like yarn, similar hues woven together, intertwined pieces of the same fabric, being added to over time. And I'm a randomly selected piece of cloth, sewn on to cover a hole. I can spend my life wondering where the cloth is that I match with and let it guide me one way. I can also choose to accept things as they are with gratitude." I'm focusing on a bee hovering outside the window, and it bumps the glass before flying off. I smile a little and look back to Dr. Cho, who's listening intently. "...But I'm not willing to sacrifice who I am and who I want to become for acceptance anymore. I've found so many amazing friends here, and I feel like we get each other. On this whole different level." My hands wave in the air around my head. "I want to be part of something bigger, like Moon's activist work. And I want to learn more about the history of my country. I want to get in contact with groups that are looking into international adoption reform. I want to speak out against racism and police brutality. I want equal rights for all people, of all colors, of all ages, genders, and sexual orientations. I want to care about things that are bigger than myself!" I'm nearly shouting. "I want to have conversations that are hard to have because they're necessary and relevant. I've never wanted anything before now, but I want the things I do to make a difference. I can use my place in this world to be a bridge. To bring awareness to my Caucasian friends and family about issues they don't know even exist. And to bring awareness to the Asian community that there are Asians out there with no roots in the foundation of their culture. But that doesn't make us white, that doesn't make us other, that makes us people that need to be embraced even more by both communities. And to be accepted! I want to build a better world for my future kids. For all the future kids!" I smile. "I found my people here," I say with a small laugh as a tear forms in my eye. "I found who I belong with. My purpose. I think maybe you fixed me."

After a short pause, Dr. Cho replies, "You did this, Van, you got yourself here," she stands and embraces me, rubbing my back. "You should be so proud of yourself. Look at where you are now compared to where you started! You've grown so much, and I couldn't be more honored to be part of your life."

She releases me, and we sit again before I tell her, "I've decided I'm not going back to my job."

Dr. Cho chuckles, "Isn't that the whole reason you came here?"

"Yeah," I smile sheepishly. "I came here to keep my job. But it was like, fate, right? This was destiny?"

"What? That you came here in order to keep your job? You made a lot of self-discoveries and see a clear path ahead of you now? And that gives you the courage to leave something familiar? And you couldn't have discovered all this had you not feared losing something that doesn't matter in the first place?" She questions, sarcastically teasing.

I laugh loudly and toss a cream throw pillow at her from the couch beside me.

"Seriously!" I snort, "You couldn't have just told me all this in the beginning and saved me thirty days of my life?" I joke.

"You wouldn't have listened," she smiles, "You have to learn these things for yourself."

And I feel like everything is connected, and everything I've experienced has created something in me, making me exactly who I am today. And I held this power inside of me all along. I just had to go on this journey to find it.

End Quote

It was nearly time for breakfast to end, and I apologize to Dr. Cho, telling her I promised everyone I would be at breakfast. She rises quickly and rushes over to search for something under some papers on her desk.

"I have a gift for you. Just something small to mark your accomplishments."

She hands me a small rectangular package wrapped in shimmering white paper with a golden Korean dragon dancing across it. The thin sheet crinkles as I pull the tape loose with a slide of my finger. As I hold the familiar weight of the book-shaped item in my hand, I fold back a corner of the wrapping to reveal a red leatherbound journal with the name *Vanessa* stamped on it. I pulle it free, and Dr. Cho takes the wrapping paper from me. I turn it over, then open it and flip through the beige pages with empty deep rust-colored lines. Inside the front cover is a handwritten note.

***

Keep writing, Van! You have a voice that screams to be heard. Find a way to tell the stories that need to be told. Speak for the people who don't have a voice. Be strong. Be Brave. Be true. Keep fighting! I will always be here if you ever need a break. But while you're out in the world, experience everything and write it down.

jasin-I doelmankeum yong-gamhaela
(Be brave enough to be yourself)

Odessa Cho

***

I look up from the page and snap the book closed before my tears fall and ruin the pages.

"Thank you," I say, hugging her tightly.

"It's been my pleasure to be your therapist, Van," she says, and we release our embrace. "You'd better get going, though, only ten minutes left for breakfast."

I wipe my eyes with my sleeve as I speed walk down the hallway leading to the main entrance. I rush to get to our usual table. Completely skipping grabbing anything to eat.

"Hey!" I say breathlessly, pulling out a chair.

"Hey! There you are!" Sunni chirps.

"What's up, graduate?" Dakk hi-fives me.

"Saved something for you," Moon says, shoving a plate of bacon and cold biscuits and gravy toward me.

"Oh my God, thank you," I say before inhaling a piece of bacon whole. Dangling it above my face and ungracefully maneuvering my open mouth to try to catch it.

"We going to hit up group?" Raafe asks. "Or ditch and just hang out outside until you have to go?"

"What time is your Uber coming?" Ajay questions.

"Ten-fif-ty," I get out through a mouth full of hard biscuit and gravy.

"It's up to you," Moon winks, "No pressure."

I swallow and reply, "I have to go to class to graduate. And I promised Emma I would finish. I already missed a lot of time being bummed out. So, we should go to class. It'll be my last Asian support group before I go unsupported into the big wide world."

We all laugh, and Kate snatches my plate away as I swipe to grab the last pieces of bacon off it.

"Oh my God," she whines, "we need to be there like now!"

We all get up and start walking, then catching the time on the clock, unanimously break into a sprint to get to our Asian group. We rush through the interlinking hallways until we reach the Plum one. Everyone slows and begins fixing themselves before the six of us stroll in, interrupting everything.

"What a bunch of dicks we are," I laugh to everyone under my breath.

"We sorry!" Dakk's voice breaks through the quiet of the room. His hands are up as he though he's approaching armed guards.

And the rest of us emerge from behind him through the doorway.

"Sorry," we each say as we find an open chair. Sheepish expressions showing our embarrassment for the disrespect.

There are several new faces I don't recognize in group today. Most of them were ghostly pale, and they have their eyes lowered, searching the floor.

The group leader is explaining the importance of punctuality. Going on about how structure is therapeutic and how breaking a schedule can be traumatic for some. I stop listening. I'm scrolling through the days here in my mind. Watching myself during my first groups. Remembering that I was nothing like them. They're sitting here scared but in control. I didn't have that control. I was terrified of my fear. They were the brave ones. They were here fighting with nothing but faith that things can only get better.

I glance over at Kate and Sunni, sitting with their legs crisscrossed under them on the cushions on the floor. Leaning lazily up against the wall behind the circle of chairs. They're giggling at something the other just said. And the laughter in their eyes makes me smile. I find Ajay's warm eyes, and he smiles at me, then focuses back on the group leader. I see Dakk pulling his flat-billed baseball hat off and using the same hand to scratch the back of his head before saying.

"C'mon, man, we apologize. It's not like we ever done this before. One time." He's holding his index finger straight up, baseball hat still in hand.

I'm trying to stifle my laughter, but I can't keep my face from smiling.

"Let's move ooooooooon," Moon's saying through cupped hands around his mouth. "It's Van's last day, for Christ's sake. Let's gooooooo."

I feel everyone's gaze turn and focus on me.

"Oh wonderful!" the leader claps his hands together and holds them that way as he continues, "Vanessa would you like to share first today? Maybe tell everyone a little bit about what you've learned during your time here?"

"Suuure," I hiss out, feeling the heat rising up my neck and creeping up into my cheeks. I'm embarrassed because I'm unprepared. Wondering how I couldn't have seen this coming. I can feel the small vibration of panic stirring deep inside. My heartbeat pounding loudly in thumps under my throat. There's a slick layer of sweat lining my palms, and I move my line of sight over to Moon as I wipe them hard on my jeans.

His eyes are dark, the color of espresso. And he smiles at me before mouthing, 'You got this!' and nodding at me.

I look back at the leader, whose face is lit up with anticipation. I close my eyes and take a deep breath in and let it out. Feeling my heart slow a little. I think of Emma and how I have someone waiting for me out there, and I feel my courage returning. I think of Brella and of all the ways I will work to fix the system that ended up breaking her. I will devote my days to fighting for everyone out there like her. And this strength allows me to open my eyes.

I stand and reach my hand out, asking the leader for the new member card in his hand.

"It's the least I can do. It's my last day, and I refused to do it on my first day, remember? I kinda owe it to you to use the card once." I smile.

He looks confused and thrilled at the same time and holds it out to me.

I take in everyone's faces. Really looking at every single one. Fucking beautiful, strong, fierce people. And I was one of them.

I let my gaze fall to the card in my hand, scrolling across the words briefly before taking one more deep breath.

"Hello, my name is Van. I am…"

I look up.

NOTE FROM AUTHOR

The Ones Who Misbehave was a passion project inspired by the 2020 Covid-19 Pandemic. During the earliest stages of the pandemic, a rise in hate crimes targeting Asian Americans began. This was due to the terms like "Kung Flu" and "China Virus," which told societies worldwide that this virus should be blamed on anyone that appeared Eastern Asian. I wrote this book as a plea to bring awareness to those who may not realize or understand the racism that Asians have endured. I wanted to speak about racism that occurs between all racial groups and the misunderstandings that can deteriorate our society. We must change our way of thinking before the world will change. We do not fight racism with racism.

TheHannaLeeWrites.com

THE ONES WHO MISBEHAVE

Made in the USA
Columbia, SC
23 August 2022

65945392R00105